Paul Leland Haworth

George Washington: Farmer

Paul Leland Haworth

George Washington: Farmer

1st Edition | ISBN: 978-3-75236-035-6

Place of Publication: Frankfurt am Main, Germany

Year of Publication: 2020

Outlook Verlag GmbH, Germany.

GEORGE WASHINGTON:

FARMER

By

PAUL LELAND HAWORTH

PREFACE

The story of George Washington's public career has been many times told in books of varying worth, but there is one important aspect of his private life that has never received the attention it deserves. The present book is an attempt to supply this deficiency.

I desire to acknowledge gratefully the assistance I have received from Messrs. Gaillard Hunt and John C. Fitzpatrick of the Library of Congress, Mr. Hubert B. Fuller lately of Washington and now of Cleveland, Colonel Harrison H. Dodge and other officials of the Mount Vernon Association, and from the work of Paul Leicester Ford, Worthington C. Ford and John M. Toner.

Above all, in common with my countrymen, I am indebted to heroic Ann Pamelia Cunningham, to whose devoted labor, despite ill health and manifold discouragements, the preservation of Mount Vernon is due. To her we should be grateful for a shrine that has not its counterpart in the world—a holy place that no man can visit without experiencing an uplift of heart and soul that makes him a better American.

PAUL LELAND HAWORTH.

CHAPTER I

A MAN IN LOVE WITH THE SOIL

One December day in the year 1788 a Virginia gentleman sat before his desk in his mansion beside the Potomac writing a letter. He was a man of fifty-six, evidently tall and of strong figure, but with shoulders a trifle stooped, enormously large hands and feet, sparse grayish-chestnut hair, a countenance somewhat marred by lines of care and marks of smallpox, withal benevolent and honest-looking—the kind of man to whom one could intrust the inheritance of a child with the certainty that it would be carefully administered and scrupulously accounted for to the very last sixpence.

The letter was addressed to an Englishman, by name Arthur Young, the foremost scientific farmer of his day, editor of the *Annals of Agriculture*, author of many books, of which the best remembered is his *Travels in France* on the eve of the French Revolution, which is still read by every student of that stirring era.

"The more I am acquainted with agricultural affairs," such were the words that flowed from the writer's pen, "the better I am pleased with them; insomuch, that I can no where find so great satisfaction as in those innocent and useful pursuits. In indulging these feelings I am led to reflect how much more delightful to an undebauched mind is the task of making improvements on the earth than all the vain glory which can be acquired from ravaging it, by the most uninterrupted career of conquests."

Thus wrote George Washington in the fulness of years, honors and experience. Surely in this age of crimson mists we can echo his correspondent that it was a "noble sentiment, which does honor to the heart of this truly great man." Happy America to have had such a philosopher as a father!

"I think with you that the life of a husbandman is the most delectable," he wrote on another occasion to the same friend. "It is honorable, it is amusing, and, with judicious management, it is profitable. To see plants rise from the earth and flourish by the superior skill and bounty of the laborer fills a contemplative mind with ideas which are more easy to be conceived than expressed."

The earliest Washington arms had blazoned upon it "3 Cinque foiles," which was the herald's way of saying that the bearer owned land and was a farmer.

When Washington made a book-plate he added to the old design spears of wheat to indicate what he once called "the most favorite amusement of my life." Evidently he had no fear of being-called a "clodhopper" or a "hayseed!"

Nor was his enthusiasm for agriculture the evanescent enthusiasm of the man who in middle age buys a farm as a plaything and tries for the first time the costly experiment of cultivating the soil. He was born on a plantation, was brought up in the country and until manhood he had never even seen a town of five thousand people. First he was a surveyor, and so careful and painstaking was he that his work still stands the test. Later he became a soldier, and there is evidence to show that at first he enjoyed the life and for a time had military ambitions. When Braddock's expedition was preparing he chafed at the prospect of inaction and welcomed the offer to join the general's staff, but the bitter experiences of the next few years, when he had charge of the herculean task of protecting the settlers upon the "cold and Barren Frontiers ... from the cruel Incursions of a crafty Savage Enemy," destroyed his illusions about war. After the capture of Fort Duquesne had freed Virginia from danger he resigned his commission, married and made a home. Soon after he wrote to an English kinsman who had invited him to visit London: "I am now I believe fixed at this seat with an agreeable Consort for Life. And hope to find more happiness in retirement than I ever experienced amidst a wide bustling world."

Thereafter he quitted the quiet life always with reluctance. Amid long and trying years he constantly looked forward to the day when he could lay down his burden and retire to the peace and freedom of Mount Vernon, there to take up again the task of farming. As Commander-in-Chief of the Armies of the Revolution and as first President of the Republic he gave the best that was in him—and it was always good enough—but more from a sense of duty than because of any real enthusiasm for the rôle of either soldier or statesman. We can well believe that it was with heartfelt satisfaction that soon after independence was at last assured he wrote to his old comrade-in-arms the Marquis de Chastellux: "I am at length become a private citizen on the banks of the Potomac, where under my own vine and fig-tree free from the bustle of a camp and the intrigues of a court, I shall view the busy world with calm indifference, and with serenity of mind, which the soldier in pursuit of glory, and the statesman of a name, have not leisure to enjoy."

Years before as a boy he had copied into a wonderful copy-book that is still preserved in the Library of Congress some verses that set forth pretty accurately his ideal of life—an ideal influenced, may we not believe, in those impressionable years by these very lines. These are the verses—one can not call them poetry—just as I copied them after the clear boyish hand from the

4

time-yellowed page:

TRUE HAPPINESS

These are the things, which once possess'd
Will make a life that's truly bless'd
A good Estate on healthy Soil,
Not Got by Vice nor yet by toil;
Round a warm Fire, a pleasant Joke,
With Chimney ever free from Smoke:
A strength entire, a Sparkling Bowl,
A quiet Wife, a quiet Soul,
A Mind, as well as body, whole
Prudent Simplicity, constant Friend,
A Diet which no art Commends;
A Merry Night without much Drinking
A happy Thought without much Thinking;
Each Night by Quiet Sleep made Short
A Will to be but what thou art:
Possess'd of these, all else defy
And neither wish nor fear to Die
  These are things, which once Possess'd
  Will make a life that's truly bless'd.

George Washington did not affect the rôle of a Cincinnatus; he took it in all sincerity and simpleness of heart because he loved it.

Nor was he the type of farmer—of whom we have too many—content to vegetate like a lower organism, making scarcely more mental effort than one of his own potatoes, parsnips or pumpkins. As the pages that follow will reveal, he was one of the first American experimental agriculturists, always alert for better methods, willing to take any amount of pains to find the best fertilizer, the best way to avoid plant diseases, the best methods of cultivation, and he once declared that he had little patience with those content to tread the ruts their fathers trod. If he were alive to-day, we may be sure that he would be an active worker in farmers' institutes, an eager visitor to agricultural colleges, a reader of scientific reports and an enthusiastic promoter of anything tending to better American farming and farm life.

CHAPTER II

BUILDING AN ESTATE

Augustine Washington was a planter who owned thousands of acres of land, most of it unimproved, besides an interest in some small iron works, but he had been twice married and at his death left two broods of children to be provided for. George, a younger son—which implied a great deal in those days of entail and primogeniture—received the farm on the Rappahannock on which his father lived, amounting to two hundred and eighty acres, a share of the land lying on Deep Run, three lots in Frederick, a few negro slaves and a quarter of the residuary estate. He was also given a reversionary interest in Mount Vernon, bequeathed to his half-brother Lawrence. The total value of his inheritance was small, and, as Virginia landed fortunes went, he was left poorly provided for.

Much of Washington's youth was spent with Lawrence at Mount Vernon, and as an aside it may be remarked here that the main moulding influence in his life was probably cast by this high-minded brother, who was a soldier and man of the world. By the time he was sixteen the boy was on the frontier helping Lord Thomas Fairfax to survey the princely domain that belonged to his lordship, and received in payment therefor sometimes as much as a doubloon a day. In 1748 he patented five hundred fifty acres of wild land in Frederick County, "My Bullskin Plantation" he usually called it, payment being made by surveying. In 1750 he had funds sufficient to buy four hundred fifty-six acres of land of one James McCracken, paying therefor one hundred twelve pounds. Two years later for one hundred fifteen pounds he bought five hundred fifty-two acres on the south fork of Bullskin Creek from Captain George Johnston. In 1757 he acquired from a certain Darrell five hundred acres on Dogue Run near Mount Vernon, paying three hundred fifty pounds.

It is evident, therefore, that very early he acquired the "land hunger" to which most of the Virginians of his day were subject, as a heritage from their English ancestry. In the England of that day, in fact, no one except a churchman could hope to attain much of a position in the world unless he was the owner of land, and until the passage of the great Reform Bill in 1832 he could not even vote unless he held land worth forty shillings a year. In Virginia likewise it was the landholder who enjoyed distinction and consideration, who was sent to the House of Burgesses and was bowed and scraped to as his coach bumped along over the miserable roads. The movement to cities did not begin until after the Industrial Revolution, and people still held the healthy notion that the country was the proper place in which to live a normal human existence.

In 1752 Lawrence Washington died. As already stated, he was the proprietor by inheritance of Mount Vernon, then an estate of two thousand five hundred acres which had been in the Washington family since 1674, being a grant from Lord Culpeper. Lawrence had fought against the Spaniards in the conflict sometimes known as the war of Jenkins's Ear, and in the disastrous siege of Cartagena had served under Admiral Vernon, after whom he later named his estate. He married Anne Fairfax, daughter of Sir William Fairfax, and for her built

Mount Vernon, Showing Kitchen to the Left and Covered Way Leading to It.

From a painting by T.P. Rossiter and L.R. Mignot **The Washington Family.**

on his estate a new residence, containing eight rooms, four to each floor, with a large chimney at each end.

Lawrence Washington was the father of four children, but only an infant daughter, Sarah, survived him, and she died soon after him. By the terms of his father's and Lawrence's wills George Washington, after the death of this child, became the ultimate inheritor of the Mount Vernon estate, but, contrary to the common idea, Anne Fairfax Washington, who soon married George Lee, retained a life interest. On December 17, 1754, however, the Lees executed a deed granting said life interest to George Washington in consideration of an annual payment during Anne Lee's lifetime of fifteen thousand pounds of tobacco or the equivalent in current money[1]. Mrs. Lee died in 1761 and thereafter Washington owned the estate absolutely. That it was by no means so valuable at that time as its size would indicate is shown by the smallness of the, rent he paid, never more than four hundred sixty-five dollars a year. Many eighty-acre farms rent for that much to-day and even for more.

[1] From entries in Washington's account book we know that this
equivalent in 1755 was £93.15; during each of the next four years it was
£87.10, and for 1760 it was £81.5.

Up to 1759 Washington was so constantly engaged in fighting the French and Indians that he had little time and opportunity to look after his private affairs and in consequence they suffered. In 1757 he wrote from the Shenandoah Valley to an English agent that he should have some tobacco to sell, but could not say whether he did have or not. His pay hardly sufficed for his personal expenses and on the disastrous Fort Necessity and Braddock campaigns he lost his horses and baggage. Owing to his absence from home, his affairs fell into great disorder from which they were extricated by a fortunate stroke.

This stroke consisted in his marriage to Martha Custis, relict of the wealthy Daniel Parke Custis. The story of his wooing the young widow has been often told with many variations and fanciful embellishments, but of a few facts we are certain. From a worldly point of view Mrs. Custis was the most desirable woman in all Virginia, and the young officer, though not as yet a victor in many battles, had fought gallantly, possessed the confidence of the Colony and formed a shining exception to most of the tidewater aristocracy who continued to hunt the fox and guzzle Madeira while a cruel foe was harrying the western border. Matters moved forward with the rapidity traditional in similar cases and in about three weeks and before the Colonel left to join Forbes in the final expedition against Fort Duquesne the little widow had been wooed and won. After his return from that expedition Washington resigned his commission and on the 6th of January, 1759, they were married at her "White House" on York River and spent their honeymoon at her "Six Chimney House" in Williamsburg.

The young groom and farmer—as he would now have styled himself—was at this time not quite twenty-seven years old, six feet two inches high, straight as an Indian and weighed about one hundred and seventy-five pounds. His bones and joints were large, as were his hands and feet. He was wide-shouldered but somewhat flat-chested, neat-waisted but broad across the hips, with long arms and legs. His skin was rather pale and colorless and easily burned by the sun, and his hair, a chestnut brown, he usually wore in a queue. His mouth was large and generally firmly closed and the teeth were already somewhat defective. His countenance as a whole was pleasing, benevolent and commanding, and in conversation he looked one full in the face and was deliberate, deferential and engaging. His voice was agreeable rather than strong. His demeanor at all times was composed and dignified, his movements and gestures graceful, his walk majestic and he was a superb horseman[2].

[2] Adapted from a description written by his comrade-in-arms, George Mercer.

The bride brought her husband a "little progeny" consisting of two interesting stepchildren; also property worth about a hundred thousand dollars, including many negro slaves, money on bond and stock in the Bank of England. Soon we find him sending certificates of the marriage to the English agents of the Custis estate and announcing to them that the management of the whole would be in his hands.

The dower negroes were kept separate from those owned by himself, but otherwise he seems to have made little distinction between his own and Mrs. Washington's property, which was now, in fact, by Virginia law his own. When Martha wanted money she applied to him for it. Now and then in his cash memorandum books we come upon such entries as, "By Cash to Mrs. Washington for Pocket Money £4." As a rule, if there were any purchases to be made, she let George do it and, if we may judge from the long list of tabby colored velvet gowns, silk hose, satin shoes, "Fashionable Summer Cloaks & Hatts," and similar articles ordered from the English agents she had no reason to complain that her husband was niggardly or a poor provider. If her "Old Man"—for she sometimes called him that—failed in anything she desired, tradition says that the little lady was in the habit of taking hold of a button of his coat and hanging on until he had promised to comply.

He managed the property of the two children with great care and fidelity, keeping a scrupulous account in a "marble colour'd folio Book" of every penny received or expended in their behalf and making a yearly report to the general court of his stewardship. How minute this account was is indicated by an entry in his cash memorandum book for August 21, 1772: "Charge Miss

Custis with a hair Pin mended by C. Turner" one shilling. Her death (of "Fitts") in 1773 added about ten thousand pounds to Mrs. Washington's property, which meant to his own.

There can be no question that the fortune he acquired by the Custis alliance proved of great advantage to him in his future career, for it helped to make him independent as regards money considerations. He might never have become the Father of His Country without it. Some of his contemporaries, including jealous-hearted John Adams, seem to have realized this, and tradition says that old David Burnes, the crusty Scotsman who owned part of the land on which the Federal City was laid out, once ventured to growl to the President: "Now what would ye ha' been had ye not married the widow Custis?" But this was a narrow view of the matter, for Washington was known throughout the Colonies before he married the Custis pounds sterling and was a man of too much natural ability not to have made a mark in later life, though possibly not so high a one. Besides, as will be explained in detail later, much of the Custis money was lost during the Revolution as a result of the depreciation in the currency.

Following his marriage Washington added largely to his estate, both in the neighborhood of Mount Vernon and elsewhere. In 1759 he bought of his friend Bryan Fairfax two hundred and seventy-five acres on Difficult Run, and about the same time from his neighbor, the celebrated George Mason of Gunston Hall, he acquired one hundred acres next that already bought of Darrell. Negotiations entered into with a certain Clifton for the purchase of a tract of one thousand eight hundred six acres called Brents was productive of much annoyance. Clifton agreed in February, 1760, to sell the ground for one thousand one hundred fifty pounds, but later, "under pretence of his wife not consenting to acknowledge her right of dower wanted to disengage himself ... and by his shuffling behavior convinced me of his being the trifling body represented." Washington heard presently that Clifton had sold the land to another man for one thousand two hundred pounds, which fully "unravelled his conduct ... and convinced me that he was nothing less than a thorough paced rascal." Ultimately Washington acquired Brents, but had to pay one thousand two hundred ten pounds for it.

During the next few years he acquired other tracts, notably the Posey plantation just below Mount Vernon and later often called by him the Ferry Farm. With it he acquired a ferry to the Maryland shore and a fishery, both of which industries he continued.

By 1771 he paid quit rents upon an estate of five thousand five hundred eighteen acres in Fairfax County; on two thousand four hundred ninety-eight acres in Frederick County; on one thousand two hundred fifty acres in King

George; on two hundred forty in Hampshire; on two hundred seventy-five in Loudoun; on two thousand six hundred eighty-two in Loudoun Faquier—in all, twelve thousand four hundred sixty-three acres. The quit rent was two shillings and sixpence per hundred acres and amounted to £15.11.7.

In addition to these lands in the settled parts of Virginia he also had claims to vast tracts in the unsettled West. For services in the French and Indian War he was given twenty thousand acres of wild land beyond the mountains—a cheap mode of reward, for the Ohio region was to all intents and purposes more remote than Yukon is to-day. Many of his fellow soldiers held their grants so lightly that he was able to buy their claims for almost a song. The feeling that such grants were comparatively worthless was increased by the fact that to become effective they must be located and surveyed, while doubt existed as to whether they would be respected owing to conflicting claims, jurisdictions and proclamations.

Washington, however, had seen the land and

The Porter's Lodge.

Driveway from the Lodge Gate.

11

knew it was good and he had prophetic faith in the future of the West. He employed his old comrade Captain William Crawford to locate and survey likely tracts not only in what is now West Virginia and western Pennsylvania, but beyond the Ohio River. Settlement in the latter region had been forbidden by the King's proclamation of 1763, but Washington thought that this was merely a temporary measure designed to quiet the Indians and was anxious to have picked out in advance "some of the most valuable land in the King's part." In other words he desired Crawford to act the part of a "Sooner," in the language of more than a century later.

In this period a number of companies were scrambling for western lands, and Washington, at one time or another, had an interest in what was known as the Walpole Grant, the Mississippi Company, the Military Company of Adventurers and the Dismal Swamp Company. This last company, however, was interested in redeeming lands about Dismal Swamp in eastern Virginia and it was the only one that succeeded. In 1799 he estimated the value of his share in that company at twenty thousand dollars.

Washington took the lead in securing the rights of his old soldiers in the French War, advancing money to pay expenses in behalf of the common cause and using his influence in the proper quarters. In August, 1770, he met many of his former officers at Captain Weedon's in Fredericksburg, and after they had dined and had talked over old times, they discussed the subject of their claims until sunset, and it was decided that Washington should personally make a long and dangerous trip to the western region.

In October he set out with his old friend Doctor James Craik and three servants, including the ubiquitous Billy Lee, and on the way increased the party. They followed the old Braddock Road to Pittsburgh, then a village of about twenty log cabins, visiting en route some tracts of land that Crawford had selected. At Pittsburgh they obtained a large dugout, and with Crawford, two Indians and several borderers, floated down the Ohio, picking out and marking rich bottom lands and having great sport hunting and fishing.

The region in which they traveled was then little known and was unsettled by white men. Daniel Boone had made his first hunting trip into "the dark and bloody ground of Kaintuckee" only the year before, and scattered along the banks of the Ohio stood the wigwam villages of the aboriginal lords of the land. At one such village Washington met a chief who had accompanied him on his memorable winter journey in 1753 to warn out the French, and elsewhere talked with Indians who had shot at him in the battle of the Monongahela and now expressed a belief that he must be invulnerable. At the Mingo Town they saw a war party of three score painted Iroquois on their way to fight the far distant Catawbas. Between the Indians and the white men peace nominally reigned, but rumors were flying of impending uprisings, and the Red Man's smouldering hate was soon to burst into the flame known as Lord Dunmore's War. Once the party was alarmed by a report that the Indians had killed two white men, but they breathed easier on learning that the sole basis of the story was that a trader had tried to swim his horse across the Ohio and had been drowned. In spite of uncertainties, the voyagers continued to the Great Kanawha and paddled about fourteen miles up that stream. Near its mouth Washington located two large tracts for himself and military comrades and after interesting hunting experiences and inspecting some enormous sycamores—concerning which matters more hereafter—the party turned back, and Washington reached home after an absence of nine weeks.

Two of Washington's western tracts are of special interest. One had been selected by Crawford in 1767 and was "a fine piece of land on a stream called Chartiers Creek" in the present Washington County, southwest of Pittsburgh. Crawford surveyed the tract and marked it by blazed trees, built four cabins and cleared a patch of ground, as an improvement, about each. Later Washington, casting round for some one from whom to obtain a military title with which to cover the tract, bought out the claim of his financially embarrassed old neighbor Captain John Posey to three thousand acres, paying £11.11.3, or about two cents per acre. Crawford, now a deputy surveyor of the region, soon after resurveyed two thousand eight hundred thirteen acres and forwarded the "return" to Washington, with the result that in 1774 Governor Dunmore of Virginia granted a patent for the land.

In the meantime, however, six squatters built a cabin upon the tract and cleared two or three acres, but Crawford paid them five pounds for their improvements and induced them to move on. To keep off other interlopers he placed a man on the land, but in 1773 a party of rambunctious Scotch-Irishmen appeared on the scene, drove the keeper away, built a cabin so close in front of his door that he could not get back in, and continued to hold the land until after the Revolution.

By that time Crawford himself was dead—having suffered the most terrible of all deaths—that of an Indian captive burnt at the stake.

The other tract whose history it is worth our while to follow consisted of twelve hundred acres on the Youghiogheny River, likewise not far from Pittsburgh. It bore seams of coal, which Washington examined in 1770 and thought "to be of the very best kind, burning freely and abundance of it." In the spring of 1773 he sent out a certain Gilbert Simpson, with whom he had formed a sort of partnership, to look after this land, and each furnished some laborers, Washington a "fellow" and a "wench." Simpson managed to clear some ground and get in six acres of corn, but his wife disliked life on the borderland and made him so uncomfortable with her complaints that he decided to throw up the venture. However, he changed his mind, and after a trip back East returned and, on a site noticed by the owner on his visit, built a grist mill on a small stream now called Washington's Run that empties into the Youghiogheny. This was one of the first mills erected west of the Alleghany Mountains and is still standing, though more or less rebuilt. The millstones were dug out of quarries in the neighborhood and the work of building the mill was done amid considerable danger from the Indians, who had begun what is known as Dunmore's War. Simpson's cabin and the slave quarters stood near what is now Plant No. 2 of the Washington Coal and Coke Company. The tract of land contains valuable seams of coal and with some contiguous territory is valued at upward of twenty million dollars.

Washington had large ideas for the development of these western lands. At one time he considered attempting to import Palatine Germans to settle there, but after careful investigation decided that the plan was impracticable. In 1774 he bought four men convicts, four indented servants, and a man and his wife for four years and sent them and some carpenters out to help Simpson build the mill and otherwise improve the lands. Next year he sent out another party, but Indian troubles and later the Revolution united with the natural difficulties of the country to put a stop to progress. Some of the servants were sold and others ran away, but Simpson stayed on in charge, though without making any financial settlement with his patron till 1784.

At the close of the Revolution Washington wrote to President John Witherspoon of Princeton College that he had in the western country patents under signature of Lord Dunmore "for about 30,000 acres, and surveys for about 10,000 more, patents for which were suspended by the disputes with Great Britain, which soon followed the return of the warrants to the land office. Ten thousand acres of the above thirty lie upon the Ohio; the rest on the Great Kenhawa, a river nearly as large, and quite as easy in its navigation, as the former, The whole of it is rich bottom land, beautifully situated on these rivers, and abounding plenteously in fish, wild-fowl, and game of all kinds."

He could have obtained vast land grants for his Revolutionary services, but he stuck by his announced intention of receiving only compensation for his expenses. He continued, however, to be greatly interested in the western country and was one of the first Americans to foresee the importance of that region to the young Republic, predicting that it would become populated more rapidly than any one could believe and faster than any similar region ever had been settled. He was extremely anxious to develop better methods of communication with the West and in 1783 made a trip up the Mohawk River to the famous Oneida or Great Carrying Place to view the possibilities of waterway development in that region—the future course of the Erie Canal. Soon after he wrote to his friend the Chevalier de Chastellux: "I could not help taking a more extensive view of the vast inland navigation of these United States and could not but be struck by the immense extent and importance of it, and of the goodness of that Providence which has dealt its favors to us with so profuse a hand. Would to God we may have wisdom enough to improve them. I shall not rest contented till I have explored the Western Country, and traversed those lines or great part of them, which have given bounds to a new empire."

In partnership with George Clinton he bought, in 1784, a tract of six thousand acres on the Mohawk, paying for his share, including interest, one thousand eight hundred seventy-five pounds. In 1793 he sold two-thirds of his half for three thousand four hundred pounds and in his will valued the thousand acres that remained at six thousand dollars. This was a speculation pure and simple, as he was never in the region in which the land lay but once.

On December 23, 1783, in an ever memorable scene, Washington resigned his commission as Commander of the Continental Army and rode off from Annapolis to Mount Vernon to keep Christmas there for the first time since 1774. The next eight months he was busily engaged in making repairs and improvements about his home estate, but on September first, having two days before said good-by to Lafayette, who had been visiting him, he set off on horseback to inspect his western lands and to obtain information requisite to a scheme he had for improving the "Inland Navigation of the Potomac" and connecting its head waters by canal with those of the Ohio. The first object was rendered imperative by the settlement of squatters on part of his richest land, some of which was even being offered for sale by unscrupulous land agents.

With him went again his old friend Doctor Craik. Their equipage consisted of three servants and six horses, three of which last carried the baggage, including a marquee, some camp utensils, a few medicines, "hooks and lines," Madeira, port wine and cherry bounce. Stopping at night and for meals at taverns or the homes of relatives or friends, they passed up the picturesque Potomac Valley, meeting many friends along the way, among them the celebrated General Daniel Morgan, with whom Washington talked over the waterways project. At "Happy Retreat," the home of Charles Washington in the fertile Shenandoah Valley, beyond the Blue Ridge, Washington met and transacted business with tenants who lived on his lands in that region. On September fifth he reached Bath, the present Berkeley Springs, where he owned two thousand acres of land and two lots. Here fifteen years before he had come with his family in the hope that the water would benefit poor "Patey" Custis, and here he met "the ingenious Mr. Rumney" who showed him the model of a boat to be propelled by steam.

At Bath the party was joined by Doctor Craik's son William and by the General's nephew, Bushrod Washington. Twelve miles to the west Washington turned aside from the main party to visit a tract of two hundred forty acres that he owned on the Virginia side of the Potomac. He found it "exceedingly Rich, & must be very valuable—the lower end of the Land is rich white oak in places springey … the upper part is … covered with Walnut of considerable size many of them." He "got a snack" at the home of a Mr. McCracken and left with that gentleman the terms upon which he would let the land, then rode onward and rejoined the others.

The cavalcade passed on to Fort Cumberland. There Washington left the main party to follow with the baggage and hurried on ahead along Braddock's old road in order to fill an appointment to be at Gilbert Simpson's by the fifteenth. Passing through the dark tangle of Laurel known as the Shades of Death, he came on September twelfth to the opening among the mountains—the Great Meadows—where in 1754 in his rude little fort of logs, aptly named Fort Necessity, he had fought the French and had been conquered by them. He owned the spot now, for in 1770 Crawford had bought it for him for "30 Pistols[3]," Thirty years before, as an enthusiastic youth, he had called it a "charming field for an encounter"; now he spoke of it as "capable of being turned to great advantage … a very good stand for a Tavern—much Hay may be cut here When the ground is laid down in grass & the upland, East of the Meadow, is good for grain."

[3] Doubtless he meant pistoles, coins, not weapons.

Not a word about the spot's old associations!

The same day he pushed on through the mountains, meeting "numbers of Persons & Pack horses going in with Ginseng; & for Salt & other articles at the Markets below," and near nightfall reached on the Youghiogheny River the tract on which Gilbert Simpson, his agent, lived. He found the land poorer than he had expected and the buildings that had been erected indifferent, while the mill was in such bad condition that "little Rent, or good is to be expected from the present aspect of her," He was, in fact, unable to find a renter for the mill and let the land, twelve hundred acres, now worth millions, for only five hundred bushels of wheat!

The land had cost him far more than he had received from it. Simpson had not proved a man of much energy and even had he been otherwise conditions in the region would have prevented him from accomplishing much in a financial way, for there was little or no market for farm produce near at hand and the cost of transportation over the mountains was prohibitive. During the Revolution, however, Simpson had in some way or other got hold of some paper currency and a few months before had turned over the worthless bills to Washington. A century later the package was sold at auction, and the band, which was still unbroken, bore upon it in Washington's hand: "Given by Gilbt. Simpson, 19 June, 1784."

At Simpson's Washington was met by a delegation from the squatters on his holdings on Miller's Run or Chartiers Creek, "and after much conversation & attempts in them to discover all the flaws they could in my Deed &c." they announced that they would give a definite answer as to what they would do when Washington reached the land in dispute.

He drew near the neighborhood on the following Saturday, but the next day "Being Sunday, and the People living on my Land, *apparently* very religious, it was thought best to postpone going among them till to-morrow." On Monday, in company with several persons including the high sheriff, Captain Van Swearingen, or "Indian Van," captain of one of the companies in Morgan's famous rifle corps, he proceeded to the land and found that, of two thousand eight hundred thirteen acres, three hundred sixty-three were under cultivation and forty more were in meadow. On the land stood twelve cabins and nine barns claimed by fourteen different persons, most or all of whom were doughty Scotch-Irishmen.

Washington was humane enough to see that they had something to urge in their behalf and offered to sell them the whole tract at twenty-five shillings an acre, or to take them as tenants, but they stubbornly refused his offers and after much wrangling announced their intention to stand suit. Ejectment proceedings were accordingly brought by Washington's attorney, Thomas Smith of Carlisle. The case was tried in 1786 before the Supreme Court of Pennsylvania and resulted in Washington's favor.

In 1796 Washington sold the tract to a certain Matthew Richey for twelve thousand dollars, of which three thousand one hundred eighty dollars was to be paid in cash and the rest in three annual instalments. Richey died in 1798, and Washington's heirs had difficulties in their attempts to collect the remainder.

Leaving these legal matters to be disposed of by lawyers, Washington turned back without visiting his Kanawha or Ohio lands, and on October fourth reached Mount Vernon, having traveled on horseback about six hundred eighty miles. One result of his trip was the formation of the Potomac Company,

The Seed House, Beyond Lay the Vegetable Garden.

One of the Artificial Mounds. The Tree upon It was Set out by Mrs. Grover Cleveland.

but this is a subject that lies without the scope of this book.

From that time onward he bought occasional tracts of lands in various parts of the country or acquired them in discharge of debts. By the death of his mother he acquired her land on Accokeek Creek in Stafford County, near where his father had operated an iron furnace.

Washington's landed estate as listed in his will amounted to about sixty thousand two hundred two acres, besides lots in Washington, Alexandria, Winchester, Bath, Manchester, Edinburgh and Richmond. Nine thousand two hundred twenty-seven acres, including Mount Vernon and a tract on Four Mile Run, he specifically bequeathed to individuals, as he did some of the lots. The remaining lots and fifty thousand nine hundred seventy-five acres (some of which land was already conditionally sold) he directed to be disposed of, together with his live stock, government bonds and shares held by him in the Potomac Company, the Dismal Swamp Company, the James River Company and the banks of Columbia and Alexandria—the whole value of which he conservatively estimated at five hundred and thirty thousand dollars. The value of the property he specifically bequeathed, with his slaves, which he directed should be freed, can only be guessed at, but can hardly have been short of two hundred and twenty thousand dollars more. In other words, he died possessed of property worth three-quarters of a million and was the richest man in America.

Not all of the land that he listed in his will proved of benefit to his heirs. The title to three thousand fifty-one acres lying on the Little Miami River in what is now Ohio and valued by him at fifteen thousand two hundred fifty-five dollars proved defective. In 1790 a law, signed by himself, had passed Congress requiring the recording of such locations with the federal Secretary of State. Washington's locations and surveys of this Ohio land had already been recorded in the Virginia land office, and with a carelessness unusual in him he neglected to comply with the statute. After his death certain persons took advantage of the defect and seized the lands, and his executors failed to embrace another opportunity given them to perfect the title, with the result that the lands were lost.

The matter rested until a few years ago when some descendants of the heirs set their heads together and one of them, Robert E. Lee, Jr., procured his appointment in 1907 by the court of Fairfax County as administrator *de bonis non* of Washington's estate. It was, of course, impossible to regain the lands—which lie not far from Cincinnati and are worth vast sums—so the movers in the matter had recourse to that last resort of such claimants—Congress—and, with the modesty usually shown by claimants, asked that body to reimburse the heirs in the sum of three hundred and five thousand one hundred dollars—that is, one hundred dollars per acre—with interest from the date of petition.

Thus far Congress has not seen fit to comply, nor does there seem to be any good reason why it should do so. The land cost Washington a mere bagatelle, it was lost through the neglect of himself and his executors, and not one of the persons who would benefit by such a subsidy from the public funds is his lineal descendant. As a mere matter of public policy and common sense it may well be doubted whether any claim upon government, no matter how just in itself, should be reimbursed beyond the third generation. The heirs urge in extenuation of the claim that Washington refused to accept any compensation for his Revolutionary services, but it is answered that it is hardly seemly for his grand nephews and grand nieces many times removed to beg for something that the Father of His Country himself rejected. One wonders whether the claimants would dare to press their claims in the presence of their great Kinsman himself!

CHAPTER III

VIRGINIA AGRICULTURE IN WASHINGTON'S DAY

The Virginia of George Washington's youth and early manhood was an imperial domain reaching from Atlantic tidewater through a thousand leagues of forests, prairies and mountains "west and northwest" to the South Sea. Only a narrow fringe along the eastern coast was settled by white men; the remainder was a terra incognita into which Knights of the Golden Horseshoe and Indian traders had penetrated a short distance, bringing back stories of endless stretches of wolf-haunted woodland, of shaggy-fronted wild oxen, of saline swamps in which reposed the whitened bones of prehistoric monsters, of fierce savage tribes whose boast was of the number of scalps that swung in the smoke of their wigwams. Even as late as 1750 the fertile Shenandoah Valley beyond the Blue Ridge formed the extreme frontier, while in general the "fall line," where the drop from the foothills to the coastal plain stops navigation, marked the limit of settlement.

At the time that Washington began to farm in earnest eastern Virginia had, however, been settled for one hundred fifty-two years. Yet the population was almost wholly rural. Williamsburg, the capital, was hardly more than a country village, and Norfolk, the metropolis, probably did not contain more than five thousand inhabitants. The population generally was so scattered that, as has been remarked, a man could not see his neighbor without a telescope or be heard by him without firing a gun.

A large part of the settled land was divided up into great estates, though there were many small farms. Some of these estates had been acquired for little or nothing by Cavalier favorites of the colonial governors. A few were perfectly enormous in size, and this was particularly the rule on the "Northern Neck," the region in which Mount Vernon was situated. The holding of Lord Thomas Fairfax, the early friend and patron of Washington, embraced more than a score of modern counties and contained upward of five million acres. The grant had been made by Fairfax's grandfather, Lord Culpeper, the coproprietor and Governor of Virginia.

The Virginia plantation of 1760 was much more sufficient unto itself than was the same plantation of the next century when methods of communication had improved, articles from the outside world were easier to obtain, and invention was beginning to become "the mother of necessity." Many of the large plantations, in fact, bore no small resemblance to medieval manors. There was the planter himself residing with his family in the mansion, which corresponded to the manor house, and lording it over a crowd of white and black dependents, corresponding to serfs. The servants, both white and black, dwelt somewhat apart in the quarters, rude log huts for the most part, but probably as comfortable as those of the Saxon churls of the time of the Plantagenets. The planter's ownership over the persons of his dependents was, however, much more absolute than was that of the Norman lord, for on the manors the serfs could not be sold off the land, a restriction that did not apply in Virginia either to black slaves or indentured servants. On the manor, furthermore, the serf had his own bits of ground, for which he paid rent in kind, money or service, and the holdings passed from father to son; on the plantation the slave worked under an overseer on his master's crops only and had nothing that he could call his own—not even his wife or children. In the matter of the organization of industries there was a closer resemblance. The planter generally raised the staple articles of food for his family and slaves, as did the lord, and a large proportion of the other articles used or consumed were manufactured on the place. A son of George Mason, Washington's close friend and neighbor, has left us the following description of industry at Gunston Hall:

"My father had among his slaves carpenters, coopers, sawyers, blacksmiths, tanners, curriers, shoemakers, spinners, weavers, and knitters, and even a distiller. His woods furnished timber and plank for the carpenters and coopers, and charcoal for the blacksmith; his cattle killed for his own consumption and for sale, supplied skins for the tanners, curriers, and shoemakers; and his sheep gave wool and his fields produced cotton and flax for the weavers and spinners, and his own orchards fruit for the distillers. His carpenters and sawyers built and kept in repair all the dwelling-houses, barns, stables, ploughs, harrows, gates, etc., on the plantations, and the outhouses of the house. His coopers made the hogsheads the tobacco was prized in, and the tight casks to hold the cider and other liquors. The tanners and curriers, with the proper vats, etc., tanned and dressed the skins as well for upper as for lower leather to the full amount of the consumption of the estate, and the shoemakers made them into shoes for the negroes. A professed shoemaker was hired for three or four months in the year to come and make up the shoes for the white part of the family. The blacksmiths did all the iron work required by the establishment, as making and repairing ploughs, harrows, teeth, chains, bolts, etc. The spinners, weavers, and knitters made all the coarse cloths and stockings used by the negroes, and some of fine texture worn by the white family, nearly all worn by the children of it. The distiller made every fall a good deal of apple, peach, and persimmon brandy. The art of distilling from

21

grain was not then among us, and but few public distilleries. All these operations were carried on at the home house, and their results distributed as occasion required to the different plantations. Moreover, all the beeves and hogs for consumption or sale were driven up and slaughtered there at the proper seasons, and whatever was to be preserved was salted and packed away for distribution."

Nevertheless the plantation drew upon the outside world for many articles, especially luxuries, and the owner had to find the wherewithal to make payment. The almost universal answer to this problem was—tobacco. It was not an ideal answer, and historians have scolded the departed planters vigorously for doing the sum in that way, yet the planters were victims of circumstances. They had no gold or silver mines from which to draw bullion that could be coined into cash; the fur trade was of little importance compared with that farther north; the Europe of that day raised sufficient meat and grain for its own use, and besides these articles were bulky and costly to transport. But Europe did have a strong craving for the weed and, almost of necessity, Virginians set themselves to satisfying it. They could hardly be expected to do otherwise when a pound of tobacco would often bring in England more than a bushel of wheat, while it cost only a sixtieth part as much to send it thither. It is estimated that prior to the Revolution Virginia often sent out annually as much as ninety-six thousand hogsheads of tobacco. Tobacco took the place of money, and debts, taxes and even ministers' salaries were paid in it.

The disadvantages of tobacco culture are well known. Of all crops it is perhaps the most exhausting to the soil, nor was a large part of Virginia particularly fertile to begin with. Much land was speedily ruined, but nothing was so cheap and plentiful in that day as land, so the planter light-heartedly cleared more and let the old revert to the wilderness. Any one who travels through the long settled parts of Virginia to-day will see many such old fields upon which large forest trees are now growing and can find there, if he will search closely enough, signs of the old tobacco ridges. Only heroic measures and the expenditure of large sums for fertilizer could make such worn-out land again productive. Washington himself described the character of the agriculture in words that can not be improved upon:

"A piece of land is cut down, and left under constant cultivation, first in tobacco, and then in Indian corn (two very exhausting plants), until it will yield scarcely anything; a second piece is cleared, and treated in the same manner; then a third and so on, until probably there is but little more to clear. When this happens, the owner finds himself reduced to the choice of one of three things—either to recover the land which he has ruined, to accomplish which, he has perhaps neither the skill, the industry, nor the means; or to retire beyond the mountains; or to substitute quantity for quality in order to raise something. The latter has been generally adopted, and, with the assistance of horses, he scratches over much ground, and seeds it, to very little purpose."

The tobacco industry was not only ruinous to the soil, but it was badly organized from a financial standpoint. Three courses were open to the planter who had tobacco. He might sell it to some local mercantile house, but these were not numerous nor as a rule conveniently situated to the general run of planters. He might deposit it in a tobacco warehouse, receiving in return a receipt, which he could sell if he saw fit and could find a purchaser. Or he could send his tobacco direct to an English agent to be sold.

If a great planter and particularly if situated upon navigable water, this last was the course he was apt to follow. He would have his own wharf to which once or twice a year a ship would come bringing the supplies he had ordered months before and taking away the great staple. If brought from a distance, the tobacco was rarely hauled to the wharf in wagons—the roads were too wretched for that—instead it was packed in a great cylindrical hogshead through which an iron or wooden axle was put. Horses or oxen were then hitched to the axle and the hogshead was rolled to its destination.

By the ship that took away his tobacco the planter sent to the English factor a list of the goods he would require for the next year. It was an unsatisfactory way of doing business, for time and distance conspired to put the planter at the factor's mercy. The planter was not only unlikely to obtain a fair price for his product, but he had to pay excessive prices for poor goods and besides could never be certain that his order would be properly filled.

Washington's experiences with his English agents were probably fairly typical. Near the close of 1759 he complained that Thomas Knox of Bristol had failed to send him various things ordered, such as half a dozen scythes and stones, curry combs and brushes, weeding and grubbing hoes, and axes, and that now he must buy them in America at exorbitant prices. Not long afterward he wrote again: "I have received my goods from the Recovery, and cant help again complaining of the little care taken in the purchase: Besides leaving out half and the most material half too! of the Articles I sent for, I find the Sein is without Leads, corks and Ropes which renders it useless—the crate of stone ware don't contain a third of the Pieces I am charged with, and only two things broken, and everything very high Charged."

In September of the same year he ordered, among other things, busts of Alexander the Great, Julius Caesar, Charles XII of Sweden, Frederick the Great, Prince Eugene and the Duke of Marlborough; also of two wild beasts. The order was "filled" by sending him a group showing Aeneas bearing his father from Troy, two groups with two statues of Bacchus and Flora, two ornamental vases and two "Lyons."

"It is needless for me to particularise the sorts, quality, or taste I woud choose to have them in unless it is observd," he wrote a year later to Robert Gary & Company of London apropos of some articles with which he was dissatisfied, "and you may believe me when I tell you that instead of getting things good and fashionable in their several kind, we often have articles sent us that coud only have been used by our Forefathers in the days of yore—'Tis a custom, I have some reason to believe, with many Shop keepers, and Tradesmen in London when they know Goods are bespoke for Transportation to palm sometimes old, and sometimes very slight and indifferent goods upon us taking care at the same time to advance 10, 15, or perhaps 20 pr. Ct. upon them."

To his London shoemaker he wrote, November 30, 1759, that the last two pairs of dog leather pumps scarce lasted twice as many days. To his tailor he complained on another occasion of exorbitant prices. "I shall only refer you generally to the Bills you have sent me, particularly for a Pompadour Suit forwarded last July amounting to £16.3.6 without embroidery, Lace or Binding—not a close fine cloth neither—and only a gold Button that woud not stand the least Wear."

Another time he mentions that his clothes fit poorly, which is not strange considering that measurements had to be sent three thousand miles and there, was no opportunity to try the garments on with a view to alterations. We may safely conclude, therefore, that however elegant Virginia society of that day may have been in other respects, it was not distinguished for well fitting clothes!

Most Virginia planters got in debt to their agents, and Washington was no exception to the rule. When his agents, Robert Gary & Company, called his attention to the fact, he wrote them, that they seemed in a bit of a hurry considering the extent of past dealings with each other. "Mischance rather than Misconduct hath been the cause of it," he asserted, explaining that he had made large purchases of land, that crops had been poor for three seasons and prices bad. He preferred to let the debt stand, but if the agents insisted upon payment now he would find means to discharge the obligation.

Not all planters could speak so confidently of their ability to find means to discharge a debt, for the truth is that the profits of tobacco culture were by no means so large as has often been supposed. A recent writer speaks of huge incomes of twenty thousand to eighty thousand pounds a year and asserts that "the ordinary planter could count on an income of from £3,000 to £6,000." The first figures are altogether fabulous, "paper profits" of the same sort that can be obtained by calculating profits upon the geometrical increase of geese as illustrated in a well known story. Even the last mentioned sums were realized only under the most favorable conditions and by a few planters. Much of the time the price of the staple was low and the costs of transportation and insurance, especially in time of war, were considerable. Washington himself had a consignment of tobacco captured by the French.

The planters were by no means so prosperous as is often supposed and neither was their life so splendid as has often been pictured. Writers seem to have entered into a sort of conspiracy to mislead us concerning it. The tendency is one to which Southern writers are particularly prone in all that concerns their section. If they speak of a lawyer, he is always a profound student of the law; of a soldier, he is the bravest tenderest knight that ever trod shoe leather; of a lady, she is the most beautiful that ever graced a drawing-room.

The old Virginia life had its color and charm, though its color and charm lay in large part in things concerning which the writers have little or nothing to say. It is true that a few planters had their gorgeous coaches, yet Martha Washington remembered when there was only one coach in the whole of Virginia, and throughout her life the roads were so wretched that those who traveled over them in vehicles ran in imminent danger of being overturned, with possible dislocation of limbs and disjointing of necks. Virginians had their liveried servants, mahogany furniture, silver plate, silks and satins; an examination of the old account books proves that they often had these and many other expensive things, along with their Madeira and port wine. But the same books show that the planter was chronically in debt and that bankruptcy was common, while accounts left by travelers reveal the fact that many of the mansion houses were shabby and run down, with rotting roofs, ramshackle doors, broken windows into which old hats or other garments had been thrust to keep the wind away. In a word, a traveler could find to-day more elegance in a back county of Arkansas than then existed in tidewater Virginia.

The tobacco industry was a culture that required much labor. In the spring a pile of brush was burned and on the spot thus fertilized and made friable the seed were sowed. In due course the ground was prepared and the young plants were transplanted into rows. Later they must be repeatedly plowed, hoed and otherwise cultivated and looked after and finally

By permission of the Mount Vernon Ladies' Association **The Mount Vernon Kitchen (restored).**

the leaves must be cut or gathered and carried to the dry house to be dried. One man could care for only two or three acres, hence large scale cultivation required many hands—result, the importation of vast numbers of indentured servants and black slaves, with the blighting effects always consequent upon the presence of a servile class in a community.

Although tobacco was the great staple, some of the Virginia planters had begun before the Revolution to raise considerable crops of wheat, and most of them from the beginning cultivated Indian corn. From the wheat they made flour and bread for themselves, and with the corn they fed their hogs and horses and from it also made meal for the use of their slaves. In the culture of neither crop were they much advanced beyond the Egyptians of the times of the Pyramids. The wheat was reaped with sickles or cradles and either flailed out or else trampled out by cattle and horses, usually on a dirt floor in the open air. Washington estimated in 1791 that the average crop of wheat amounted to only eight or ten bushels per acre, and the yield of corn was also poor.

So much emphasis was laid upon tobacco that many planters failed to produce food enough. Some raised none at all, with the result that often both men and animals were poorly fed, and at best the cost of food and forage exhausted most of the profits. A somewhat similar condition exists in the South to-day with regard to cotton.

Almost no attention was paid to conserving the soil by rotation of crops, and even those few planters who attempted anything of the sort followed the old plan of allowing fields to lie in a naked fallow and to grow up in noxious weeds instead of raising a cover crop such as clover. Washington wrote in 1782: "My countrymen are too much used to corn blades and corn shucks; and have too little knowledge of the profit of grass land." And again in 1787:

"The general custom has been, first to raise a crop of Indian corn (maize) which, according to the mode of cultivation, is a good preparation for wheat; then a crop of wheat; after which the ground is respited (except for weeds, and every trash that can contribute to its foulness) for about eighteen months; and so on, alternately, without any dressing, till the land is exhausted; when it is turned out, without being sown with grass-seeds, or reeds, or any method taken to restore it; and another piece is ruined in the same manner. No more cattle is raised than can be supported by lowland meadows, swamps &c. and the tops and blades of Indian corn; as very few persons have attended to growing grasses, and connecting cattle with their crops. The Indian corn is the chief support of the labourers and their horses."

As for the use of fertilizer, very little was attempted, for, as Jefferson explained, "we can buy an acre of new land cheaper than we can manure an old one." It was this cheapness of land that made it almost impossible for the Virginians to break away from their ruinous system—ruinous, not necessarily to themselves, but to future generations. Conservation was then a doctrine that was little preached. Posterity could take care of itself. Only a few persons like Washington realized their duty to the future.

In the matter of stock as well as in pure agriculture the Virginians were backward. They showed to best advantage in the matter of horses. Virginia gentlemen were fond of horses, and some owned fine animals and cared for them carefully. A Randolph of Tuckahoe is said to have had a favorite dapple-gray named "Shakespeare" for whom he built a special stable with a sort of recess next the stall in which the groom slept. Generally speaking, however, even among the aristocracy the horses were not so good nor so well cared for as in the next century.

Among the small farmers and poorer people the horses were apt to be scrubs, often mere bags of bones. A scientific English agriculturist named Parkinson, who came over in 1798, tells us that the American horses generally "leap well; they are accustomed to leap from the time of foaling; as it is not at all uncommon, if the mare foal in the night, for some part of the family to ride the mare, with the foal following her, from eighteen to twenty miles next day, it not being customary to walk much. I think that is the cause of the American horse having a sort of amble: the foal from its weak state, goes pacing after the dam, and retains that motion all its life. The same is the case with respect to leaping: there being in many places no gates, the snake or worm-fence (which is one rail laid on the end of another) is taken down to let the mare pass through, and the foal follow: but, as it is usual to leave two or three rails untaken down, which the mare leaps over, the foal, unwilling to be left behind, follows her; so that, by the time it is one week old, it has learned to leap three feet high; and progressively, as it grows older, it leaps higher, till at a year old, it will leap its own height."

Sheep raising was not attempted to any great extent, partly because of the ravages of wolves and dogs and partly because the sheep is a perverse animal that often seems to prefer dying to keeping alive and requires skilled care to be made profitable. The breeds were various and often were degenerated. Travelers saw Holland or rat-tailed sheep, West Indian sheep with scant wool and much resembling goats, also a few Spanish sheep, but none would have won encomiums from a scientific English breeder. The merino had not yet been introduced. Good breeds of sheep were difficult to obtain, for both the English and Spanish governments forbade the exportation of such animals and they could be obtained only by smuggling them out.

In 1792 Arthur Young expressed astonishment when told that wolves and dogs were a serious impediment to sheep raising in America, yet this was undoubtedly the case. The rich had their foxhounds, while every poor white and many negroes had from one to half a dozen curs—all of which canines were likely to enjoy the sport of sheep killing. Mr. Richard Peters, a well informed farmer of Pennsylvania, said that wherever the country was much broken wolves were to be found and bred prodigiously. "I lay not long ago at the foot of South Mountain, in York county, in this State, in a country very thickly settled, at the house of a Justice of the Peace. Through the night I was kept awake by what I conceived to be a jubilee of dogs, assembled to bay the moon. But I was told in the morning, that what disturbed me, was *only* the common howling of wolves, which nobody there regarded. When I entered the *Hall of Justice*, I found the 'Squire giving judgment for the reward on two wolf whelps a countryman had taken from the bitch. The *judgment-seat* was shaken with the intelligence, that the wolf was coming—*not to give bail*—but to devote herself or rescue her offspring. The animal was punished for this *daring contempt*, committed in the face of the court, and was shot within a hundred yards of the tribunal."

Virginians had not yet learned the merits of grass and pasture, and their cattle, being compelled to browse on twigs and weeds, were often thin and poor. Many ranged through the woods and it was so difficult to get them up that sometimes they would not be milked for two or three days. Often they gave no more than a quart of milk a day and were probably no better in appearance than the historian Lecky tells us were the wretched beasts then to be found in the Scottish Highlands.

Hogs received even less care than cattle and ran half wild in the woods like their successors, the famous Southern razor-backs of to-day, being fed only a short period before they were to be transformed into pork. Says Parkinson:

"The real American hog is what is termed the wood-hog: they are long in the leg, narrow on the back, short in the body, flat on the sides, with a long snout, very rough in their hair, in make more like a fish called a perch than anything I can describe. You may as well think of stopping a crow as those hogs. They will go a distance from a fence, take a run, and leap through the rails, three or four feet from the ground, turning themselves sidewise. These hogs suffer such hardships as no other animal could endure. It is customary to keep them in the woods all winter, as there is no thrashing or fold-yards; and they must live on the roots of trees, or something of that sort, but they are poor beyond any creature that I ever saw. That is probably the cause why American pork is so fine. They are something like forest-sheep. I am not certain, with American keeping and treatment, if they be not the best: for I never saw an animal live without food, except this; and I am pretty sure they nearly do that. When they are fed, the flesh may well be sweet: it is all young, though the pig be ten years old."

"The aim of the farmers in this country (if they can be called farmers)," wrote Washington to Arthur Young in 1791, "is, not to make the most they can from the land, which is or has been cheap, but the most of the labour, which is dear; the consequence of which has been, much ground has been *scratched* over and none cultivated or improved as it ought to have been: whereas a farmer in England, where land is dear, and labour cheap, finds it his interest to improve and cultivate highly, that he may reap large crops from a small quantity of ground."

No clearer statement of the differences between American and European agriculture has ever been formulated. Down to our own day the object of the American farmer has continued to be the same—to secure the largest return from the expenditure of a given amount of labor. But we are on the threshold of a revolution, the outcome of which means intensive cultivation and the realization of the largest possible return from a given amount of land.

That Washington saw the distinction so clearly is of itself sufficient proof that he pondered long and deeply upon agricultural problems.

CHAPTER IV

WASHINGTON'S PROBLEM

"No estate in United America," wrote Washington to Arthur Young in 1793, "is more pleasantly situated than this. It lies in a high, dry, and healthy country, 300 miles by water from the sea, and, as you will see by the plan, on one of the finest rivers in the world. Its margin is washed by more than ten miles of tide water; from the beds of which and the innumerable coves, inlets, and small marshes, with which it abounds, an inexhaustible fund of mud may be drawn as a manure, either to be used separately or in a compost....

"The soil of the tract of which I am speaking is a good loam, more inclined, however, to clay than sand. From use, and I might add, abuse, it is become more and more consolidated, and of course heavier to work....

"This river, which encompasses the land the distance above mentioned, is well supplied with various kinds of fish at all seasons of the year; and, in the spring, with great profusion of shad, herring, bass, carp, perch, sturgeon, etc. Several fisheries appertain to the estate; the whole shore, in short, is one entire fishery."

The Mount Vernon estate, amounting in the end to over eight thousand acres, was, with the exception of a few outlying tracts, subdivided into five farms, namely, the Mansion House Farm, the Union Farm, the Dogue Run Farm, Muddy Hole Farm and the River Farm.

On the Mansion House Farm stood the owner's residence, quarters for the negroes and other servants engaged upon that particular estate, and other buildings. The land in general was badly broken and poor in quality; much of it was still in woodland.

The River Farm lay farthest up the Potomac, being separated from the others by the stream known as Little Hunting Creek. Visitors to Mount Vernon to-day, traveling by trolley, cross this farm and stream. It contained more tillable ground than any other, about twelve hundred acres. In 1793 it had an "overlooker's" house of one large and two small rooms below and one or two rooms above, quarters for fifty or sixty negroes, a large barn and stables gone much to decay.

Muddy Hole Farm lay across Little Hunting Creek from the River Farm and back of the Mansion House Farm and had no frontal upon the Potomac. It contained four hundred seventy-six acres of tillable soil and had in 1793 a small overlooker's house, "covering for about 30 negroes, and a tolerable good barn, with stables for the work-horses."

Union Farm lay just below the Mansion House Farm and contained nine hundred twenty-eight acres of arable land and meadow. In 1793 it had, in Washington's words, "a newly erected brick barn, equal, perhaps, to any in America, and for conveniences of all sorts, particularly for sheltering and feeding horses, cattle, &c. scarcely to be exceeded any where." A new house of four rooms was building, and there were quarters for fifty odd negroes. On this farm was the old Posey fishery and ferry to Maryland.

Dogue Run Farm, of six hundred fifty acres, lay back of Union Farm and upon it in 1793 stood the grist mill and later a distillery and the famous sixteen-sided "new circular barn, now finishing on a new construction; well calculated, it is conceived, for getting grain out of the straw more expeditiously than the usual mode of threshing." It had a two-room overseer's house, covering for forty odd negroes, and sheds sufficient for thirty work horses and oxen. Washington considered it much the best of all his farms. It was this farm that he bequeathed to Nelly Custis and her husband, Lawrence Lewis, and upon it they erected "Woodlawn," which is shown in the photograph herewith reproduced.

Not long since I rambled on foot over the old estate and had an opportunity to compare the reality, or what remains of it, with Washington's description. I left the Mansion House, often visited before, and strolled down the long winding drive that runs between the stunted evergreens and oaks through the old lodge gate and passed from the domain, kept trim and parklike by the Association, out upon the unkempt and vastly greater part of the old Mount Vernon.

It was early morning, about the hour when in the long past the master of the estate used to ride out on his tour of inspection. The day was one of those delicious days in early autumn when earth and sky and air and all things in nature seem kindly allied to help the heart of man leap up in gladness and to enable him to understand how there came to be a poet called Wordsworth. Meadow-larks were singing in the grass, and once in an old hedgerow over-grown with sweet-smelling wild honeysuckle I saw a covey of young quails. These hedgerows of locust and cedar are broken now, but along the old road to the mill and Pohick Church and between fields the scattered trees and now and then a bordering ditch are evidences of the old owner's handiwork.

Then and later I visited all the farms, the site of the old mill, of which only a few stones remain, the mill stream, the fishery and old ferry landing. I walked across the gullied fields and examined the soil, I noted the scanty crops they bear to-day and gained a clearer idea of what Washington's problem had been than I could have done from a library of books.

Truly the estate is "pleasantly situated," though even to-day it seems out of the world and out of the way. One must go far to find so satisfying a view as that from the old Mansion House porch across the mile of shining water to the Maryland hills' crowned with trees glorified by the Midas-touch of frost. The land does lie "high" and "dry," but we must take exception to the word "healthy." In the summer and fall the tidal marshes breed a variety of mosquito capable of biting through armor plate and of infecting the devil himself with malaria. In the General's day, when screens were unknown, a large part of the population, both white and black, suffered every August and September from chills and fever. The master himself was not exempt and once we find him chronicling that he went a-hunting and caught a fox and the ague.

What he says as regards the fisheries is all quite true and in general they seem to have been very productive. Herring and shad were the chief fish caught and when the run came the seine was carried well out into the river in a boat and then hauled up on the shelving beach either by hand or with a windlass operated by horse-power. There were warehouses and vats for curing the fish, a cooper shop and buildings for sheltering the men. The fish were salted down for the use of the family and the slaves, and what surplus remained was sold. Now and then the landing and outfit was rented out for a money consideration, but this usually happened only when the owner was away from home.

At the old Posey fishery on Union Farm the industry is still carried on, though gasoline engines have been substituted for the horse-operated winch used in drawing the seines. Lately the industry has ceased to be very productive, and an old man in charge told me that it is because fishermen down the river and in Chesapeake Bay are so active that comparatively few fish manage to get up so far.

The Mount Vernon estate in the old days lacked only one quality necessary to make it extremely productive, namely, rich soil! Only ignorance of what good land really is, or an owner's blind pride in his own estate, can justify the phrase "a good loam." On most of the estate the soil is thin, varying in color from a light gray to a yellow red, with below a red clay hardpan almost impervious to water. To an observer brought up on a farm of the rich Middle West, Mount Vernon, except for a few scattered fields, seems extremely poor land. For farming purposes most of it would be high at thirty dollars an acre. Much of it is so broken by steep hills and deep ravines as scarcely to be tillable at all. Those tracts which are cultivated are very susceptible to erosion. Deep gullies are quickly worn on the hillsides and slopes. At one time such a gully on Union Farm extended almost completely across a large field and was deep enough to hide a horse, but Washington filled it up with trees, stumps, stones, old rails, brush and dirt, so that scarcely a trace of it was left. In places one comes upon old fields that have been allowed to revert to broom sedge, scrub oak and scrub pine. One is astonished at the amount that has never been cleared at all. Only by the most careful husbandry could such an estate be kept productive. It never could be made to yield bumper crops.

The situation confronting "Farmer Washington" was this: He had a great abundance of land, but most of it on his home estate was mediocre in quality. Some of that lying at a distance was more fertile, but much of it was uncleared and that on the Ohio was hopelessly distant from a market. With the exception of Mount Vernon even those plantations in Virginia east of the Blue Ridge could not be looked after in person. He must either rent them, trust them to a manager, or allow them to lie idle. Even the Mount Vernon land was distant from a good market, and the cost of transportation was so great that he must produce for selling purposes articles of little bulk compared with value. Finally, he had an increasing number of slaves for whom food and clothing must be provided.

His answer to the problem of a money crop was for some years the old Virginia answer—tobacco. His far western lands he left for the most part untenanted. Those plantations in settled regions but remote from his home he generally rented for a share of the crop or for cash. The staple articles that he produced to feed the slaves were pork and corn, eked out by herring from the fishery.

From his accounts we find that in 1759 he made thirty-four thousand one hundred sixty pounds of tobacco; the next year sixty-five thousand thirty-seven pounds; in 1763, eighty-nine thousand seventy-nine pounds, which appears to have been his banner tobacco crop. In 1765 the quantity fell to forty-one thousand seven hundred ninety-nine pounds; in 1771, to twenty-nine thousand nine hundred eighty-six pounds, and in 1773 to only about five thousand pounds. Thereafter his crop of the weed was negligible, though we still find occasional references to it even as late as 1794, when he states that he has twenty-five hogsheads in the warehouses of Alexandria, where he has held it for five or six years because of low prices.

He tried to raise a good quality and seems to have

Looking across part of Dogue Run Farm to "Woodlawn," the Home of Nelly Custis Lewis).

Gully on a Field of Union Farm, Showing Susceptibility to Erosion.

concentrated on what he calls the "sweet scented" variety, but for some reason, perhaps because his soil was not capable of producing the best, he obtained lower prices than did some of the other Virginia planters, and grumbled at his agents accordingly.

He early realized the ruinous effects of tobacco on his land and sought to free himself from its clutches by turning to the production of wheat and flour for the West India market. Ultimately he was so prejudiced against the weed that in 1789 we find him in a contract with a tenant named Gray, to whom he leased a tract of land for ten pounds, stipulating that Gray should make no more tobacco than he needed for "chewing and smoking in his own family."

Late in life he decided that his land was not congenial to corn, in which he was undoubtedly right, for the average yield was only about fifteen bushels per acre. In the corn country farmers now often produce a hundred. He continued to raise corn only because it was essential for his negroes and hogs.

In 1798 he contracted with William A. Washington to supply him with five hundred barrels annually to eke out his own crop. Even this quantity did not prove sufficient, for we find him next year trying to engage one hundred barrels more.

Before this time his main concern had come to be to conserve his soil and he had turned his attention largely to grass and live stock. Of these matters more hereafter.

CHAPTER V

THE STUDENT OF AGRICULTURE

Washington took great pains to inform himself concerning any subject in which he was interested and hardly was he settled down to serious farming before he was ordering from England "the best System now extant of Agriculture," Shortly afterward he expressed a desire for a book "lately published, done by various hands, but chiefly collected from the papers of Mr. Hale. If this is known to be the best, pray send it, but not if any other is in high esteem." Another time he inquires for a small piece in octavo, "a new system of Agriculture, or a speedy way to grow rich."

Among his papers are preserved long and detailed notes laboriously taken from such works as Tull's *Horse-Hoeing Husbandry*, Duhamel's *A Practical Treatise of Husbandry, The Farmer's Compleat Guide,* Home's *The Gentleman Farmer*, and volumes of Young's *Annals of Agriculture.*

The abstracts from the *Annals* were taken after the Revolution and probably before he became President, for the first volume did not appear until 1784. From the handwriting it is evident that the digests of Tull's and Duhamel's books were made before the Revolution and probably about 1760. In the midst of the notes on chapter eight of the *Compleat Guide* there are evidences of a long hiatus in time—Mr. Fitzpatrick of the manuscript division of the Library of Congress thinks perhaps as much as eight or ten years. A vivid imagination can readily conceive Washington's laying aside the task for the more important one of vindicating the liberties of his countrymen and taking it up again only when he had sheathed the sword. But all we can say is that for some reason he dropped the work for a considerable time, the evidence being that the later handwriting differs perceptibly from that which precedes it.

As most of Washington's agricultural ideas were drawn from these books, it is worth while for us to examine them. I have not been able to put my hands on Washington's own copies, but in the library of the Department of Agriculture I have examined the works of Tull, Duhamel and Young.

Tull's *Horse-Hoeing Husbandry* was an epoch-making book in the history of English agriculture. It was first published in 1731 and the third edition, the one I have seen and probably the one that Washington possessed, appeared in

1751. Possibly it was the small piece in octavo, "a new system of Agriculture, or a speedy way to grow rich" concerning which he wrote to his agent. It deals with a great variety of subjects, such as of roots and leaves, of food of plants, of pasture, of plants, of weeds, of turnips, of wheat, of smut, of blight, of St. Foin, of lucerne, of ridges, of plows, of drill boxes, but its one great thesis was the careful cultivation by plowing of such annuals as potatoes, turnips, and wheat, crops which hitherto had been tended by hand or left to fight their battle unaided after having once been planted.

Duhamel's book was the work of a Frenchman whose last name was Monceau. It was based in part upon Tull's book, but contained many reflections suggested by French experience as well as some additions made by the English translator. The English translation appeared in 1759, the year of Washington's marriage. It dealt with almost every aspect of agriculture and stock raising, advocated horse-hoeing, had much to say in favor of turnips, lucerne, clover and such crops, and contained plates and descriptions of various plows, drills and other kinds of implements. It also contained a detailed table of weather observations for a considerable time, which may have given Washington the idea of keeping his meteorological records.

Young's *Annals* was an elaborate agricultural periodical not unlike in some respects publications of this sort to-day except for its lack of advertising. It contains records of a great variety of experiments in both agriculture and stock raising, pictures and descriptions of plows, machines for rooting up trees, and other implements and machines, plans for the rotation of crops, and articles and essays by experimental farmers of the day. Among its contributors were men of much eminence, and we come upon articles by Mr. William Pitt on storing turnips, Mr. William Pitt on deep plowing; George III himself contributed under the pen name of "Ralph Robinson." The man who should follow its directions even to-day would not in most matters go far wrong.

As one looks over these publications he realizes that the scientific farmers of that day were discussing many problems and subjects that still interest those of the present. The language is occasionally quaint, but the principles set down are less often wrong than might be supposed. To be sure, Tull denied that different plants require different sorts of food and, notes Washington, "gives many unanswerable Reasons to prove it," but he combats the notion that the soil ever causes wheat to degenerate into rye. This he declares "as ridiculous as it would be to say that an horse by feeding in a certain pasture will degenerate into a Bull." And yet it is not difficult to discover farmers to-day who will stubbornly argue that "wheat makes cheat." Tull also advocated the idea that manure should be put on green and plowed under in order to obtain anything like its full benefit, as well as many other sound ideas that are still disregarded by many American farmers.

Washington eagerly studied the works that have been mentioned, and much of his time when at Mount Vernon was devoted to experiments designed to ascertain to what extent the principles that were sound in England could be successfully applied in an American environment.

CHAPTER VI

A FARMER'S RECORDS AND OTHER PAPERS

Washington was the most methodical man that ever lived. He had a place for everything and insisted that everything should be kept in its place. There was nothing haphazard about his methods of business. He kept exact accounts of financial dealings.

His habit of setting things down on paper was one that developed early. He kept a journal of his surveying experiences beyond the Blue Ridge in 1748, another of his trip to Barbadoes with his brother Lawrence in 1751-52, another of his trip to Fort Le Boeuf to warn out the French, and yet another of his Fort Necessity campaign. The words are often misspelled, many expressions are ungrammatical, but the handwriting is good and the judgments expressed, even those set down when he was only sixteen, are the mature judgments of a man.

A year after his marriage he began a formal diary, which he continued until June 19, 1775, the time of his appointment to command the army of the Revolution. He called it his *Diary* and later *Where, & how my time is Spent*. In it he entered the happenings of the day, his agricultural and other experiments, a record of his guests and also a detailed account of the weather.

His attention to this last matter was most particular. Often when away from home he would have a record kept and on his return would incorporate it into his book. Exactly what advantages he expected to derive therefrom are not apparent, though I presume that he hoped to draw conclusions as to the best time for planting crops. In reading it I was many times reminded of a Cleveland octogenarian who for fifty-seven years kept a record twice a day of the thermometer and barometer. Near the end of his life he brought the big ledgers to the Western Reserve Historical Society, and I happened to be present on the occasion. "You have studied the subject for a long time," I said to him. "Are there any conclusions you have been able to reach as a result of your investigation?" He thought a minute and passed a wrinkled hand across a wrinkled brow. "Nothing but this," he made answer, "that Cleveland weather is only constant in its inconstancy."

We would gladly exchange some of these meteorological details for further information about Washington's own personal doings and feelings. Of the latter the diaries reveal little. Washington was an objective man, above all in his papers. He sets down what happens and says little about causes, motives or mental impressions. When on his way to Yorktown to capture Cornwallis he visited his home for the first time in six weary years, yet merely recorded: "I reached my own Seat at Mount Vernon (distant 120 Miles from the Hd. of Elk) where I staid till the 12th."

Not a word of the emotions which that visit must have roused!

For almost six years after 1775 there is a gap in the diary, though for some months of 1780 he sets down the weather. On May I, 1781, he begins a new record, which he calls a *Journal*, and he expresses regret that he has not had time to keep one all the time. The subjects now considered are almost wholly military and the entries reveal a different man from that of 1775. The grammar is better, the vocabulary larger, the tone more elevated, the man himself is bigger and broader with an infinitely wider viewpoint.

From November 5, 1781, for more than three years there is another blank, except for the journal of his trip to his western lands already referred to. But on January 1, 1785, he begins a new *Diary* and thenceforward continues it, with short intermissions, until the day of his last ride over his estate.

A few of the diaries and journals have been lost, but most are still in existence. Some are in the Congressional Library and there also is the Toner transcript of these records. The transcript makes thirty-seven large volumes. The diary is one of the main sources from which the material for this book is drawn.

The original of the record of events for 1760 is a small book, perhaps eight or ten inches long by four inches wide and much yellowed by age. Part of the first entry stands thus:

"January 1, Tuesday

"Visited my Plantations and received an Instance of Mr. French's great Love of Money in disappointing me of some Pork because the price had risen to 22.6 after he had engaged to let me have it at 20 s."

On his return from his winter ride he found Mrs. Washington "broke out with the Meazles." Next day he states with evident disgust that he has taken the pork on French's own terms.

The weather record for 1760 was kept on blank pages of *The Virginia Almanac*, a compendium that contains directions for making "Indico," for curing bloody flux, for making "Physick as pleasant as a Dish of Chocolate," for making a striking sun-dial, also "A Receipt to keep one's self warm a whole Winter with a single Billet of Wood." To do this last "Take a Billet of

Wood of a competent Size, fling it out of the Garret-Window into the Yard, run down Stairs as hard as ever you can drive; and when you have got it, run up again with it at the same Measure of Speed; and thus keep throwing down, and fetching up, till the Exercise shall have sufficiently heated you. This renew as often as Occasion shall require. *Probatum est.*"

This receipt would seem worth preserving in this day of dear fuel. As Washington had great abundance of wood and plenty of negroes to cut it, he probably did not try the experiment—at least such a conclusion is what writers on historical method would call "a safe inference."

There is in the almanac a rhyme ridiculing

First Page of Washington's Digest of Duhamel's Husbandry.

physicians and above the March calendar are printed the touching verses:

"Thus of all Joy and happiness bereft,
And with the Charge of Ten poor Children left:
A greater Grief no Woman sure can know, Who,—
with Ten Children—who will have me now."

Also there are some other verses, very broad and "not quite the proper thing," as Kipling has it. But it must not be inferred that Washington approved of them.

Washington also kept cash memorandum books, general account books, mill books and a special book in which he recorded his accounts with the estate of the Custis children. These old books, written in his neat legible hand, are not only one of our chief sources of information concerning his agricultural and financial affairs, but contain many sidelights upon historical events. It is extremely interesting, for example, to discover in one of the account books that in 1775 at Mount Vernon he lent General Charles Lee—of Monmouth fame—£15, and "to Ditto lent him on the Road from Phila to Cambridge at different times" £9.12 more, a total of £24.12. In later years Lee intrigued against Washington and said many spiteful things about him, but he never returned the loan. The account stood until 1786, when it was settled by Alexander White, Lee's executor.

In the Cash Memorandum books we can trace Washington's military preparations at the beginning of the Revolution. Thus on June 2, 1775, being then at Philadelphia, he enters: "By Expences bringing my Horses from Baltimore," £2.5. Next day he pays thirty pounds for "Cartouch Boxes &c. for Prince Wm. Comp." June 6, "By Covering my Holsters," £0.7.6; "By a Cersingle," £0.7.6; "By 5 Books—Military," £1.12.0. He was preparing for Gage and Howe and Cornwallis and whether the knowledge contained in the books was of value or not he somehow managed for eight years to hold his opponents at bay and ultimately to win. At Cambridge, July tenth, he spends three shillings and four pence for a "Ribbon to distinguish myself," that is to show his position as commander; also £1.2.6 for "a pair of Breeches for Will," his colored body servant.

A vast number of papers bear witness to his interest in agriculture and with these we are particularly concerned. He preserved most of the letters written to him and many of these deal with farming matters. During part of his career he had a copying press and kept copies of his own important letters, while many of the originals have been preserved, though widely scattered. When away from home he required his manager to send him elaborate weekly reports containing a meteorological table of each day's weather, the work done on each farm, what each person did, who was sick, losses and increases in stock, and other matters of interest. Scores of these reports are still in existence and are invaluable. He himself wrote—generally on Sunday— lengthy weekly letters of inquiry, direction, admonition and reproof, and if the manager failed in the minutest matter to give an account of some phase of the farm work, he would be sure to hear of it in the proprietor's next letter.

Washington's correspondence on agricultural matters with Arthur Young and Sir John Sinclair, eminent English agriculturists, was collected soon after his death in a volume that is now rare. In it are a number of letters written by other American farmers, including Thomas Jefferson, relative to agriculture in their localities. These letters were the result of inquiries made of Washington by Young in 1791. In order to obtain the facts desired Washington sent out a circular letter to some of the most intelligent farmers in the Middle States, and the replies form perhaps our best source of information regarding agricultural conditions in that period.

Because of this service and of his general interest in agricultural matters Washington was elected a foreign honorary member of the English Board of Agriculture and received a diploma, which is still preserved among his papers.

Some of Washington's other agricultural papers have been printed in one form and another, but a great number, and some the most interesting, can still be consulted only in manuscript.

Washington bequeathed his books and papers, along with his Mansion House, to his nephew, Bushrod Washington, an associate justice of the Federal Supreme Court. Judge Washington failed to appreciate fully the seriousness of the obligation thus incurred and instead of safeguarding the papers with the utmost jealousy gave many, including volumes of the diary, to visitors and friends who expressed a desire to possess mementoes of the illustrious patriot. In particular he permitted Reverend William Buel Sprague, who had been a tutor in the family of Nelly Custis Lewis, to take about fifteen hundred papers on condition that he leave copies in their places. The judge also intrusted a considerable portion to the historian Jared Sparks, who issued the first considerable edition of Washington's writings. Sparks likewise was guilty of giving away souvenirs.

Bushrod Washington died in 1829 and left the papers and letter books for the most part to his nephew John Corbin Washington. In 1834 the nation purchased of this gentleman the papers of a public character, paying twenty-five thousand dollars. The owner reserved the private papers, including invoices, ciphering book, rules of civility, etc., but in 1849 sold these also to the same purchaser for twenty thousand dollars. The papers were kept for many years in the Department of State, but in the administration of Theodore Roosevelt most of them were transferred to the Library of Congress, where they could be better cared for and would be more accessible.

Bushrod Washington gave to another nephew, John Augustine Washington, the books and relics in the dining-room of the Mansion House. In course of time these were scattered, some being bought for the Boston Athenaeum, which has decidedly the larger part of Washington's library; others were purchased by the state of New York, and yet others were exhibited at the Centennial Exposition and were later sold at auction. Among the relics bought by New York was a sword wrongly said to have been sent to the General by Frederick the Great.

One hundred and twenty-seven of his letters, mostly to William Pearce, his manager at Mount Vernon during a portion of his presidency, were bought from the heirs of Pearce by the celebrated Edward Everett and now belong to the Long Island Historical Society. These have been published. His correspondence with Tobias Lear, for many years his private secretary, are now in the collection of Thomas K. Bixby, a wealthy bibliophile of St. Louis. These also have been published. The one greatest repository of papers is the Library of Congress. Furthermore, through the unwearying activities of J. M. Toner, who devoted years to the work, the Library also has authenticated copies of many papers of which it does not possess the originals.

All told, according to Mr. Gaillard Hunt, who has them in charge, the Washington manuscripts in the Library of Congress is the largest collection of papers of one person in the world. The collection contains about eighteen thousand papers in his own hand, press copies, or drafts in the writing of his secretaries, and many times that number of others. As yet all except a small part are merely arranged in chronological order, but soon it is to be sumptuously bound in royal purple levant. The color, after all, is fitting, for he was a King and he reigns still in the hearts of his countrymen.

Benjamin Franklin knew the great men of earth of his time, the princes and kings of blood royal. Near the close of his life he wrote in his will: "My fine crabtree walking-stick with a gold head, curiously wrought in the form of a cap of Liberty, I give to my friend, and the friend of mankind, General Washington. If it was a sceptre, he has merited it, and would become it."

And thus Thackeray, who knew the true from the false, the dross from pure gold: "Which was the most splendid spectacle ever witnessed, the opening feast of Prince George in London or the resignation of Washington? Which is the noble character for ages to admire—yon fribble dancing in lace and spangles, or yonder hero who sheathes his sword after a life of spotless honor, a purity unreproached, a courage indomitable, and a consummate victory? Which of these is the true gentleman? What is it to be a gentleman? Is it to have lofty aims, to lead a pure life, to keep your honor virgin; to have the esteem of your fellow-citizens, and the love of your fireside; to bear good fortune meekly; to suffer evil with constancy; and through evil or good to maintain truth always? Show me the happy man whose life exhibits these qualities, and him will we salute as gentleman, whatever his rank may be; show me the prince who possesses them, and he may be sure of our love and loyalty."

'Tis often distance only that lends enchantment, but it is Washington's proud pre-eminence that he can bear the microscope. Having read thousands of his letters and papers dealing with almost every conceivable subject in the range of human affairs, I yet feel inclined, nay compelled, to bear witness to the greatness of his heart, soul and understanding. He was human. He had his faults. He made his mistakes. But I would not detract a line from any eulogium of him ever uttered. Words have never yet been penned that do him justice.

CHAPTER VII

AGRICULTURAL OPERATIONS AND EXPERIMENTS BEFORE THE REVOLUTION

A detailed account of all of Washington's agricultural experiments would require several hundred pages and would be tedious reading. All that I shall attempt to do is to give some examples and point the way for any enthusiast to the mass of his agricultural papers in the Library of Congress and elsewhere.

At the outset it should be stated that he worked under extremely different conditions from those of to-day. Any American farmer of the present who has a problem in his head can have it solved by writing to the nearest government experiment station, a good farm paper, an agricultural college, the department of agriculture, or in some favored districts by consulting the local county "agent." Washington had no such recourse. There was not an agricultural college or agricultural paper in the whole country; the department of agriculture was not created until near the end of the next century; county "agents" were as unthought of as automobiles or electric lights; there was not a scientific farmer in America; even the Philadelphia Society for the Promotion of Agriculture was not founded until 1785. In his later years our Farmer could and did write to such foreign specialists as Arthur Young and Sir John Sinclair, but they were Englishmen unfamiliar with American soils and climate and could rarely give a weighty answer propounded to them by an American. If Washington wished to know a thing about practical farming, he usually had to find it out for himself.

This state of affairs accounts for his performing some experiments that seem absurd. Thus in the fall of 1764 we find him sowing "a few Oats to see if they would stand the winter." Any country boy of to-day could tell him that ordinary oats sown under such conditions in the latitude of Mount Vernon would winter kill too badly to be of much use, but Washington could not know it till he had tried.

In another category was his experiment in March, 1760, with lucerne. Lucerne is alfalfa. It will probably be news to most readers that alfalfa—the wonderful forage crop of the West, the producer of more gold than all the mines of the Klondike—was in use so long ago, for the impression is pretty general that it is comparatively new; the fact is that it is older than the Christian era and that the name alfalfa comes from the Arabic and means "the best crop." Evidently our Farmer had been reading on the subject, for in his diary he quotes what "Tull speaking of lucerne, says." He tried out the plant on this and several other occasions and had a considerable field of it in 1798. His success was not large with it at any time, for the Mount Vernon soil was not naturally suited to alfalfa, which thrives best in a dry and pervious subsoil containing plenty of lime, but the experiment was certainly worth trying.

In this same year, 1760, we find him sowing clover, rye, grass, hope, trefoil, timothy, spelt, which was a species of wheat, and various other grasses and vegetables, most of them to all intents and purposes unknown to the Virginia agriculture of that day.

He also recorded an interesting experiment with fertilizer. April 14, 1760, he writes in his diary:

"Mixed my composts in a box with the apartments in the following manner, viz. No. 1 is three pecks of earth brought from below the hill out of the 46 acre field without any mixture. In No. 2 is two pecks of sand earth and one of marle taken out of the said field, which marle seemed a little inclined to sand. 3 has 2 pecks of sd. earth and 1 of river sand.

"4 has a peck of Horse Dung

"5 has mud taken out of the creek

"6 has cow dung

"7 has marle from the Gulleys on the hillside, wch. seem'd to be purer than the other

"8 sheep dung

"9 Black mould from the Gulleys on the hill side, wch. seem'd to be purer than the other

"10 Clay got just below the garden

"All mixed with the same quantity and sort of earth in the most effective manner by reducing the whole to a tolerable degree of fineness and rubbing them well together on a cloth. In each of these divisions were planted three grains of wheat, 3 of oats, and as many of barley, all of equal distances in Rows and of equal depth done by a machine made for the purpose. The wheat rows are next the numbered side, the oats in the middle, and the barley on the side next the upper part of the Garden. Two or three hours after sowing in this manner, and about an hour before sunset I watered them all equally alike with water that had been standing in a tub abt two hours exposed to the sun."

Three weeks later he inspected the boxes and concluded that Nos. 8 and 9 gave the best results.

The plows of the period were cumbersome and did their work poorly. Consequently in March, 1760, Washington "Fitted a two Eyed Plow instead of a Duck Bill Plow", and tried it out, using his carriage horses in the work. But this new model proved upon the whole a failure and a little later he "Spent the greater part of the day in making a new plow of my own Invention." Next day he set the new plow to work "and found She answerd very well."

A little later he "got a new harrow made of smaller and closer teethings for harrowing in grain—the other being more proper for preparing the ground for sowing."

Much of his attention in the next few years was devoted to wheat growing, for, as already related, he soon decided gradually to discontinue tobacco and it was imperative for him to discover some other money crop to take its place. We find him steeping his seed wheat in brine and alum to prevent smut and he also tried other experiments to protect his grain from the Hessian fly and rust. Noticing how the freezing and thawing of the ground in spring often injured the wheat by lifting it out of the ground, he adopted the practice of running a heavy roller over the wheat in order to get the roots back into the ground and he was confident that when the operation was performed at the proper time, that is when the ground was soft and the roots were still alive, it was productive of good results.

In June, 1763, he "dug up abt. a load of Marle to spread over Wheat Land for experiment." In 1768 he came to the conclusion that most farmers began to cut their wheat too late, for of course cradling was a slow process—scarcely four acres per day per cradler—and if the acreage was large several days must elapse before the last of the grain could be cut, with the result that some of it became so ripe that many of the kernels were shattered out and lost before the straw could be got to the threshing floor. By careful experiments he determined that the grain would not lose perceptibly in size and weight if the wheat were cut comparatively green. In wheat-growing communities the discussion as to this question still rages—extremists on one side will not cut their wheat till it is dead ripe, while those on the other begin to harvest it when it is almost sea-green.

In 1763 Washington entered into an agreement with John Carlyle and Robert Adams of Alexandria to sell to them all the wheat he would have to dispose of in the next seven years. The price was to be three shillings and nine pence per bushel, that is, about ninety-one cents. This would not be far from the average price of wheat to-day, but, on the one side, we should bear in mind that ninety-one cents then had much greater purchasing power than now, so that the price was really much greater, and, on the other, that the cost of raising wheat was larger then, owing to lack of self-binders, threshing machines and other labor-saving devices.

The wheat thus sold by Washington was to be delivered at the wharf at Alexandria or beside a boat or flat on Four Mile Run Creek. The delivery for 1764 was 257-1/2 bushels; for 1765, 1,112-3/4 bushels; for 1766, 2,331-1/2 bushels; for 1767—a bad year—1,293-1/2 bushels; for 1768, 4,994-1/2 bushels of wheat and 4,304-1/2 bushels of corn; for 1769, 6,241-1/2 bushels of wheat.

Thereafter he ground a good part of his wheat and sold the flour. He owned three mills, one in western Pennsylvania, already referred to, a second on Four Mile Run near Alexandria, and a third on the Mount Vernon estate. This last mill had been in operation since his father's day. It was situated near the mouth of the stream known as Dogue Run, which was not very well suited for the purpose as it ran from the extreme of low water in summer to violent floods in winter and spring. Thus his miller, William A. Poole, in a letter that wins the sweepstakes in phonetic spelling, complains in 1757 that he has been able to grind but little because "She fails by want of Water." At other times the Master sallies out in the rain with rescue crews to save the mill from floods and more than once the "tumbling dam" goes by the board in spite of all efforts. The lack of water was partly remedied in 1771 by turning the water of Piney Branch into the Run, and about the same time a new and better mill was erected, while in 1797 further improvements were made. During the whole period flatboats and small schooners could come to the wharf to take away the flour. Corn and other grains were ground, as well as wheat, and the mill had considerable neighborhood custom, the toll exacted being one-eighth. Only a few stones sticking in a bank now remain of the mill.

Washington divided his flour into superfine, fine, middlings and ship stuff. It was put into barrels manufactured by the plantation coopers and much of it ultimately found its way to the West India market. A tradition—much quoted —has it that barrels marked "George Washington, Mount Vernon," were accepted in the islands without any inspection, but Mr. J.M. Toner, one of the closest students of Washington's career, contended that this was a mistake and pointed to the fact that the Virginia law provided for the inspection of all flour before it was exported and the placing of a brand on each barrel. However this may be, we have Washington's own word for it, that his flour was as good in quality as any manufactured in America—and he was no boaster.

That his flour was so good was in large measure due to the excellent quality of the wheat from which it was made. By careful attention to his seed and

Dogue Run below the Site of the Mill.

On the Road to the Mill and Pohick Church.

to cultivation he succeeded in raising grain that often weighed upward of sixty pounds to the bushel. After the Revolution he wrote: "No wheat that has ever yet fallen under my observation exceeds the wheat which some years ago I cultivated extensively."

His idea of good cultivation in these years was to let his fields lie fallow at certain intervals, though he also made use of manure, marl, etc., and in 1772 tried the experiment of sowing two bushels of salt per acre upon fallow ground, dividing the plot up into strips eight feet in width and sowing the alternate strips in order that he might be able to determine results.

He imported from England an improved Rotheran or patent plow, and, having noticed in an agricultural work mention of a machine capable of pulling up two or three hundred stumps per day, he expressed a desire for one, saying: "If the accounts are not greatly exaggerated, such powerful assistance must be of vast utility in many parts of this wooden country, where it is impossible for our force (and laborers are not to be hired here), between the finishing of one crop and preparations for another, to clear ground fast enough to afford the proper changes, either in the planting or farming business."

These were his golden days. He was not so rich as he was later nor so famous, but he was strong and well and young, he had abundant friends, and his neighbors thought well enough of him to send him to the Burgesses and to make him a vestryman of old Pohick Church; if he felt the need of recreation he went fishing or fox-hunting or attended a horse race or played a game of cards with his friends, and he had few things to trouble him seriously. But fussy kings and ministers overseas were meddling with the liberties of subjects and were creating a situation out of which was to come a mighty burden—a burden so Atalantean that it would have frightened most men, but one that he was brave enough and strong enough to shoulder and with it march down to immortality.

CHAPTER VIII

CONSERVING THE SOIL

The Revolution rudely interrupted Washington's farming experiments, and for eight long years he was so actively engaged in the grim business of checkmating Howe and Clinton and Cornwallis that he could give little time or thought to agriculture. For more than six years, in fact, he did not once set foot upon his beloved fields and heard of his crops, his servants and his live stock only from family visitors to his camps or through the pages of his manager's letters.

Peace at last brought him release. He had left Mount Vernon a simple country gentleman; he came back to it one of the most famous men in the world. He wasted no time in contemplating his laurels, but at once threw himself with renewed enthusiasm into his old occupation. His observation of northern agriculture and conversations with other farmers had broadened his views and he was more than ever progressive. He was now thoroughly convinced of the great desirability of grass and stock for conserving the soil and he was also wide awake to the need of better tools and methods and wished to make his estate beautiful as well as useful.

Much of his energy in 1784-85 was devoted to rebuilding his house and improving his grounds, and to his trip to his Ohio lands—all of which are described elsewhere. No diary exists for 1784 except that of the trip to the Ohio, but from the diary of 1785 we learn that he found time to experiment with plaster of Paris and powdered stone as fertilizers, to sow clover, orchard grass, guinea grass and peas and to borrow a scow with which to raise rich mud from the bed of the Potomac.

The growing poverty of his soil, in fact, was a subject to which he gave much attention. He made use of manure when possible, but the supply of this was limited and commercial fertilizers were unknown. As already indicated, he was beginning the use of clover and other grasses, but he was anxious to build up the soil more rapidly and the Potomac muck seemed to him a possible answer to the problem. There was, as he said, "an inexhaustible fund" of it, but the task of getting it on the land was a heavy one. Having heard of a horse-power dredge called the *Hippopotamus* that was in use on the Delaware River, he made inquiries concerning it but feared that it would not serve his purpose, as he would have to go from one hundred to eight hundred or a thousand yards from high water-mark for the mud—too far out for a horse to be available. Mechanical difficulties and the cost of getting up the mud proved too great for him—as they have proved too great even down to the present—but he never gave up the idea and from time to time tried experiments with small plots of ground that had been covered with the mud. His enthusiasm on the subject was so great that Noah Webster, of dictionary fame, who visited him in this period, says that the standing toast at Mount Vernon was "Success to the mud!"

Every scientific agriculturist knows that erosion is one of the chief causes of loss in soil fertility and that in the basins and deltas of streams and rivers there is going to waste enough muck to make all of our land rich. But the cost of getting this fertility back to the soil has thus far proved too great for us to undertake the task of restoration. It is conceivable, however, that the time may come when we shall undertake the work in earnest and then the dream of Washington will be realized.

The spring and summer of 1785 proved excessively dry, and the crops suffered, as they always do in times of drought. The wheat yield was poor and chinch bugs attacked the corn in such myriads that our Farmer found "hundreds of them & their young under the blades and at the lower joints of the Stock." By the middle of August "Nature had put on a melancholy look." The corn was "*fired* in most places to the Ear, with little appearance of yielding if Rain should now come & a certainty of making nothing if it did not."

Like millions of anxious farmers before and after him, he watched eagerly for the rain that came not. He records in his diary that on August 17th a good deal of rain fell far up the river, but as for his fields—it tantalizingly passed by on the other side, and "not enough fell here to wet a handkerchief." On the eighteenth, nineteenth and twenty-second clouds and thunder and lightning again awakened hopes but only slight sprinkles resulted. On the twenty-seventh nature at last relented and, to his great satisfaction, there was a generous downpour.

The rain was beneficial to about a thousand grains of Cape of Good Hope wheat that Washington had just sown and by the thirty-first he was able to note that it was coming up. For several years thereafter he experimented with this wheat. He found that it grew up very rank and tried cutting some of it back. But the variety was not well adapted to Virginia and ultimately he gave it up.

In this period he also tried Siberian wheat, put marl on sixteen square rods of meadow[4], plowed under rye, and experimented with oats, carrots, Eastern

Shore peas, supposed to be strengthening to land, also rib grass, burnet and various other things. He planted potatoes both with and without manure and noted carefully the difference in yields. At this time he favored planting corn in rows about ten feet apart, with rows of potatoes, carrots, or peas between. He noted down that his experience showed that corn ought to be planted not later than May 15th, preferably by the tenth or perhaps even as early as the first, in which his practice would not differ much from that of to-day. But he came to an erroneous conclusion when he decided that wheat ought to be sown in August or at the latter end of July, for this was playing into the hands of his enemy, the Hessian fly, which is particularly destructive to early sown wheat. Later he seems to have changed his mind on that point, for near the end of his life he instructed his manager to get the wheat in by September 10th. Another custom which he was advocating was that of fall and winter plowing and he had as much of it done as time and weather would permit. All of his experiments in this period were painstakingly set down and he even took the trouble in 1786 to index his agricultural notes and observations for that year.

[4] "On sixteen square rod of ground in my lower pasture, I put 140 Bushels of what we call Marle viz on 4 of these, No. Wt. corner were placed 50 bushels—on 4 others So. Wt. corner 30 bushels—on 4 others So. Et. corner 40 bushels—and on the remaining 4-20 bushels. This Marle was spread on the rods in these proportions—to try first whether what we have denominated to be Marie possesses any virtue as manure —and secondly—if it does, the quantity proper for an acre." His ultimate conclusion was that marl was of little benefit to land such as he owned at Mount Vernon.

Many of his experiments were made in what he called his "Botanical Garden," a plot of ground lying between the flower garden and the spinner's house. But he had experimental plots on most or all of his plantations, and each day as he made the rounds of his estate on horseback he would examine how his plants were growing or would start new experiments.

The record of failures is, of course, much greater than of successes, but that is the experience of every scientific farmer or horticulturist who ventures out of the beaten path. Even Burbank, the wizard, has his failures—and many of them.

One of Washington's successes was what he called a "barrel plough." At that time all seed, such as corn, wheat and oats had to be sown or dropped by hand and then covered with a harrow or a hoe or something of the kind. Washington tried to make a machine that would do the work more expeditiously and succeeded, though it should be said that his plans were not altogether original with him, as there was a plan for such a machine in Duhamel and another was published by Arthur Young about this time in the

Annals of Agriculture, which Washington was now perusing with much attention. Richard Peters also sent yet another plan.

Washington's drill, as we should call it to-day, consisted of a barrel or hollow cylinder of wood mounted upon a wheeled plow and so arranged that as the plow moved forward the barrel turned. In the barrel, holes were cut or burnt through which the corn or other seed could drop into tubes that ran down to the ground. By decreasing or increasing the number of holes the grain could be planted thicker or thinner as desired. To prevent the holes from choking up he found it expedient to make them larger on the outside than on the inside, and he also found that the machine worked better if the barrel was not kept too full of seed. Behind the drills ran a light harrow or drag which covered the seed, though in rough ground it was necessary to have a man follow after with a hoe to assist the process. A string was fastened to this harrow by which it could be lifted around when turning at the ends of the rows, the drill itself being managed by a pair of handles.

Washington wrote to a friend that the drill would not "work to good effect in land that is very full either of stumps, stones, or large clods; but, where the ground is tolerably free from these and in good tilth, and particularly in light land, I am certain you will find it equal to your most sanguine expectation, for Indian corn, wheat, barley, pease, or any other tolerably round grain, that you may wish to sow or plant in this manner. I have sown oats very well with it, which is among the most inconvenient and unfit grains for this machine.... A small bag, containing about a peck of the seed you are sowing, is hung to the nails on the right handle, and with a small tin cup the barrel is replenished with convenience, whenever it is necessary, without loss of time, or waiting to come up with the seed-bag at the end of the row."

As Washington says, the drill would probably work well under ideal conditions, but there were features of it that would incline, I have no doubt, to make its operator swear at times. There was a leather band that ran about the barrel with holes corresponding to those in the barrel, the purpose of the band being to prevent the seeds issuing out of more than one hole at the same time. This band had to be "slackened or braced" according to the influence of the atmosphere upon the leather, and sometimes the holes in the band tended to gape and admit seed between the band and the barrel, in which case Washington found it expedient to rivet "a piece of sheet tin, copper, or brass, the width of the band, and about four inches long, with a hole through it, the size of the one in the leather."

Washington was, however, very proud of the drill, and it must have worked fairly well, for he was not the man to continue to use a worthless implement simply because he had made it. He even used it to sow very small seed. In the summer of 1786 he records: "Having fixed a Roller to the tale of my drill plow, & a brush between it and the barrel, I sent it to Muddy Hole & sowed turnips in the intervals of corn[5]."

[5] Another passage from his papers in which he mentions using his drill plow is also illustrative of the emphasis he placed upon having the seed bed for a crop properly prepared. The passage describes his sowing some spring wheat and is as follows: "12th [of April, 1785].—Sowed sixteen acres of Siberian wheat, with eighteen quarts, in rows between corn, eight feet apart. This ground had been prepared in the following manner: 1. A single furrow; 2. another in the same to deepen it; 3. four furrows to throw the earth back into the two first, which made ridges of five furrows. These, being done some time ago, and the sowing retarded by frequent rains, had got hard; therefore, 4. before the seed was sown, these ridges were split again by running twice in the middle of them, both times in the same furrow; 5. after which the ridges were harrowed; and, 6. where the ground was lumpy, run a spiked roller with a harrow at the tail of it, which was found very efficacious in breaking the clods and pulverizing the earth, and would have done it perfectly, if there had not been too much moisture remaining from the late rains. After this, harrowing and rolling were necessary, the wheat was sown with the drill plough on the reduced ridges eight feet apart, as above mentioned, and harrowed in with the small harrow belonging to the plough. But it should have been observed, that, after the ridges were split by the middle double furrows, and before they were closed again by the harrow, a little manure was sprinkled in."

No man better understood the value of good clean seed than did he, but he had much trouble in satisfying his desires in this respect. Often the seed he bought was foul with weed seeds, and at other times it would not grow at all. Once he mentions having set the women and "weak hands" to work picking wild onions out of some Eastern Shore oats that he had bought.

He advocated planting the largest and finest potatoes instead of the little ones, as some farmers out of false ideas of economy still make the mistake of doing, and he followed the same principle that "the best will produce the best" in selecting all seed.

He also appreciated the importance of getting just the right stand of grain— not too many plants and not too few—upon his fields and conducted investigations along this line. He laboriously calculated the number of seed in a pound Troy of various seeds and ascertained, for example, that the number of red clover was 71,000, of timothy 298,000, of "New River Grass" 844,800 and of barley 8,925. Knowing these facts, he was able to calculate how much ought to be sowed of a given seed to the acre.

The spectacle of the former Commander of the Armies of a Continent engaging in such minute labor is ridiculous or sublime, according to the viewpoint!

In the spring of the year that he helped to frame the Federal Constitution he "Sowed the squares No. 2 & 4 at this place [Dogue Run] with oats in the following manner—viz—the East half of No. 2 with half a Bushel of Oats from George Town—and the west half with a Bushel of Poland Oats—The east half of No. 4 with half a bushel of the Poland Oats and the west half with a bushel of the George Town Oats. The objects, and design of this experiment, was to ascertn. 3 things—1st. which of these two kinds of Oats were best the George Town (which was a good kind of the common Oats)—2d. whether two or four bushels to the Acre was best—and 3d. the difference between ground dunged at the Rate of 5 load or 200 bushels to the Acre and ground undunged."

This experiment is typical of a great many others and it resulted, of course, in better yields on the manured ground and showed that two bushels of seed were preferable to four. But if he ever set down the result of the experiment as regards the varieties, the passage has escaped me.

While at Fredericksburg this year visiting his mother and his sister Betty Lewis he learned of an interesting method of raising potatoes under straw and wrote down the details in his diary. A little later when attending the Federal Convention he kept his eyes and ears open for agricultural information. He learned how the Pennsylvanians cultivated buckwheat and visited the farm of a certain Jones, who was getting good results from the use of plaster of Paris. With his usual interest in labor-saving machinery he inspected at Benjamin Franklin's a sort of ironing machine called a mangle, "well calculated," he thought, "for Table cloths & such articles as have not pleats & irregular foldings & would be very useful in large families."

This year he had in wheat seven hundred acres, in grass five hundred eighty acres, in oats four hundred acres, in corn seven hundred acres, with several hundred more in buckwheat, barley, potatoes, peas, beans and turnips.

In 1788 he raised one thousand eighty-eight bushels of potatoes on one plantation, but they were not dug till December and in consequence some were badly injured by the frost. An experiment that year was one of transplanting carrots between rows of corn and it was not successful.

He worked hard in these years, but, as many another industrious farmer has discovered, he found that he could do little unless nature smiled and fickle nature persisted in frowning. In 1785 the rain seemed to forget how to fall, and in 1786 how to stop falling. Some crops failed or were very short and soon he was so hard up that he was anxious to sell some lands or negroes to meet debts coming due. In February, 1786, in sending fifteen guineas to his mother, he wrote:

"I have now demands upon me for more than £500, three hundred and forty odd of which is due for the tax of 1786; and I know not where or when I shall receive one shilling with which to pay it. In the last two years I made no crops. In the first I was obliged to buy corn, and this year have none to sell, and my wheat is so bad I can neither eat it myself nor sell it to others, and tobacco I make none. Those who owe me money cannot or will not pay it without suits, and to sue is to do nothing; whilst my expenses, not from any extravagance, or an inclination on my part to live splendidly, but for the absolute support of my family and the visitors who are constantly here, are exceedingly high."

To bad crops were joined bad conditions throughout the country generally. The government of the Confederation was dying of inanition, America was flooded with depreciated currency, both state and Continental. In western Massachusetts a rebellion broke out, the rebels being largely discouraged debtors. A state of chaos seemed imminent and would have resulted had not the Federal Convention, of which Washington was a member, created a new government. Ultimately this government brought order and financial stability, but all this took time and Washington was so financially embarrassed in 1789 when he traveled to New York to be inaugurated President that he had to borrow money to pay the expenses of the journey.

After having set the wheels of government in motion he made an extended trip through New England and whenever public festivities would permit he examined into New England farm methods and took copious notes. On the first day up from New York he saw good crops of corn mixed with pumpkins and met four droves of beef cattle, "some of which were very fine—also a Flock of Sheep.... We scarcely passed a farm house that did not abd. in Geese." His judgment of New England stock was that the cattle were "of a good quality and their hogs large, but rather long legged." The shingle roofs, stone and brick chimneys, stone fences and cider making all attracted his attention. The fact that wheat in that section produced an average of fifteen bushels per acre and often twenty or twenty-five was duly noted. On the whole he seems to have considered the tour enjoyable and profitable in spite of the fact that on his return through Connecticut the law against Sabbath traveling compelled him to remain over Sunday at Perkins' Tavern and to attend church twice, where he "heard very lame discourses from a Mr. Pond."

About 1785 Washington had begun a correspondence with Arthur Young and also began to read his periodical called the *Annals of Agriculture*. The *Annals* convinced him more than ever of the superiority of the English system of husbandry and not only gave him the idea for some of the experiments that have been mentioned, but also made him very desirous of adopting a regular and systematic course of cropping in order to conserve his soil. Taking advantage of an offer made by Young, he ordered (August 6, 1786) through him English plows, cabbage, turnip, sainfoin, rye-grass and hop clover seed and eight bushels of winter vetches; also some months later, velvet wheat, field beans, spring barley, oats and more sainfoin seed. He furthermore expressed a wish for "a plan of the most complete and useful farmyard, for farms of about 500 acres. In this I mean to comprehend the barn, and every appurtenance which ought to be annexed to the yard."

Young was as good as his word. Although English law forbade the exportation of some of these things—a fact of which Washington was not aware—he and Sir John Sinclair prevailed upon Lord Grenville to issue a special permit and in due course everything reached Mount Vernon. Part of the seeds were somewhat injured by being put into the hold of the vessel that brought them over, with the result that they overheated—a thing that troubled Washington whenever he imported seeds—but on the whole the consignment was in fair order, and our Farmer was duly grateful.

The plows appeared excessively heavy to the Virginians who looked them over, but a trial showed that they worked "exceedingly well."

To Young's plan for a barn and barnyard Washington made some additions and constructed the barn upon Union Farm, building it of bricks that were made on the estate. He later expressed a belief that it was "the largest and most convenient one in this country." It has now disappeared almost utterly, but Young's plan was subsequently engraved in the *Annals*.

In return for the exertions of Young and Sinclair in his behalf Washington sent over some American products and also took pains to collect information for them as to the state of American agriculture. His letters show an almost pathetic eagerness to please these good friends and it is evident that in his farming operations he regarded himself as one of Young's disciples. He was no egotist who believed that because he had been a successful soldier and was now President of the United States he could not learn anything from a specialist. The trait was most commendable and one that is sadly lacking in many of his countrymen, some of whom take pride in declaring that "these here scientific fellers caint tell me nothin' about raisin' corn!"

Young and Sir John Sinclair were by no means his only agricultural correspondents. Even Noah Webster dropped his legal and philological work long enough in 1790 to propound a theory so startlingly modern in its viewpoint that it is worthy of reproduction. Said he:

"While therefore I allow, in its full extent, the value of stable manure, marl, plaster of Paris, lime, ashes, sea-weed, sea-shells & salt, in enriching land, I believe none of them are absolutely necessary, but that nature has provided an inexhaustible store of manure, which is equally accessible to the rich and the poor, & which may be collected & applied to land with very little labor and expense. This store is the *atmosphere*, & the process by which the fertilizing substance may be obtained is vegetation."

He added that such crops as oats, peas, beans and buckwheat should be raised and plowed under to rot and that land should never be left bare. As one peruses the letter he recalls that scientists of to-day tell us that the air is largely made up of nitrogen, that plants are able to "fix it," and he half expects to find Webster advocating "soil innoculation" and speaking of "nodules" and "bacteria."

Throughout the period after the Revolution our Farmer's one greatest concern was to conserve and restore his land. When looking for a new manager he once wrote that the man must be, "above all, Midas like, one who can convert everything he touches into manure, as the first transmutation toward gold; in a word, one who can bring worn-out and gullied lands into good tilth in the shortest time." He saved manure as if it were already so much gold and hoped with its use and with judicious rotation of crops to accomplish his object. "Unless some such practice as this prevails," he wrote in 1794, "my fields will be growing worse and worse every year, until the Crops will not defray the expense of the culture of them."

He drew up elaborate plans for the rotation of crops on his different farms. Not content with one plan, he often drew up several alternatives; calculated the probable financial returns from each, allowing for the cost of seed, cultivation and other expenses, and commented upon the respective advantages from every point of view of the various plans. The labor involved in such work was very great, but Washington was no shirker. He was always up before sunrise, both in winter and summer, and seems to have been so constituted that he was most contented when he had something to do. Perhaps if he had had to engage in hard manual toil every day he would have had less inclination for such employment, but he worked with his own hands only intermittently, devoting his time mostly to planning and oversight.

One such plan for Dogue Run Farm is given on the next page. To understand it the reader should bear in mind that the farm contained five hundred

No. of Fields	1793	1794	1795	1796	17
3	Corn and Potatoes	Wheat	Buckwheat for Manure	Wheat	Clov Gr
	Clover or	Corn and		Buckwheat	

4	Grass	Potatoes	Wheat	for Manure	Wh
5	Clover or Grass	Clover or Grass	Corn and Potatoes	Wheat	Buck for M
6	Clover or Grass	Clover or Grass	Clover or Grass	Corn and Potatoes	Wh
7	Wheat	Clover or Grass	Clover or Grass	Clover or Grass	Cor ₁ Pot ₂
1	Buckwheat for Manure	Wheat	Clover or Grass	Clover or Grass	Clov Gr
2	Wheat	Buckwheat for Manure	Wheat	Clover or Grass	Clov Gr

twenty-five arable acres divided into seven fields, each of which contained about seventy-five acres.

Of this rotation he noted that it "favors the land very much; inasmuch as there are but three corn crops [i.e. grain crops] taken in seven years from any field, & the first of the wheat crops is followed by a Buck Wheat manure for the second Wheat Crop, wch. is to succeed it; & which by being laid to Clover or Grass & continued therein three years will a ford much Mowing or Grassing, according as the Seasons happen to be, besides being a restoration to the Soil —But the produce of the sale of the Crops is small, unless encreased by the improving state of the fields. Nor will the Grain for the use of the Farm be adequate to the consumption of it in this Course, and this is an essential object to attend to."

In a second table he estimated the amount of work that would be required each year to carry out this plan of rotation, assuming that one plow would break up three-fourths of an acre per day. This amount is hardly half what an energetic farmer with a good team of horses will now turn over in a day with an ordinary walking plow, but the negro farmer lacked ambition, the plows were cumbersome, and much of the work was done with plodding oxen. The table follows:

	Fall	Winter	March	April	May	June	July	August	Sept.	Total
No. 3, 75 Acres—Corn and Potatoes.....	...	...	...	...	...	...	...	...	...	...
Breaking up..........	100	...	...	...	...	...	...	...	...	100
Laying off and listing	...	...	60	...	...	...	...	...	...	60
Crossing for planting.	...	...	...	10	...	...	...	...	...	10
Ploughing balks......	...	...	...	...	70	...	...	...	...	70
Crossing them........	...	...	...	...	...	70	...	...	...	70
Re-crossing	...	...	...	...	...	...	70	...	...	70
Sowing wheat	...	...	...	...	...	...	...	75	...	75
No. 4 ⎫										
No. 5 ⎬ 225 Acres—Clover or Grass........	...	...	...	...	...	...	...	...	...	...
No. 6 ⎭										
No. 1, 75 Acres—Buckwheat for Manure.	...	...	...	...	...	...	...	...	...	...
Breaking up..........	100	...	...	...	...	...	...	...	...	100
Crossing for sowing.	...	...	...	100	...	...	...	...	...	100
Ploughing it........	...	...	...	...	...	100	...	...	...	100
No. 2, 75 Acres—Wheat. Corn Ground..	...	...	...	...	...	...	...	...	...	...
No. 7, 75 Acres—Wheat or Buckwheat ..	...	...	...	...	...	...	...	100	...	100
525 Acres	200	...	60	110	70	170	70	175	...	855

PLANTING CHART.

He estimated that seventy-five acres of corn would yield, at twelve and a half bushels per acre, 937-1/2 bushels, worth at two shillings and sixpence per bushel £117.3.9. In this field potatoes would be planted between the rows of corn and would produce, at twelve and a half bushels per acre, 937-1/2 bushels, worth at one shilling per bushel £46.17.6. Two fields in wheat, a total of one hundred fifty acres, at ten bushels per acre, would yield one thousand five hundred bushels, worth at five shillings per bushel three hundred seventy-five pounds. Three fields in clover and grass and the field of buckwheat to be turned under for manure would yield no money return. In other words the whole farm would produce three thousand three hundred seventy-five bushels of grain and potatoes worth a total of £539.1.3.

A second alternative plan would yield crops worth £614.1.3; a third, about the same; a fourth, £689.1.3; a fifth, providing for two hundred twenty-five acres of wheat, £801.11.0; a sixth, £764. Number five would be most productive, but he noted that it would seriously reduce the land. Number six would be "the 2d. most productive Rotation, but the fields receive no rest," as it provided for neither grass nor pasture, while the plowing required would exceed that of any of the other plans by two hundred eighty days.

On a small scale he tried growing cotton, Botany Bay grass, hemp, white nankeen grass and various other products. He experimented with deep soil plowing by running twice in the same furrow and also cultivated some wheat that had been drilled in rows instead of broadcasted.

In 1793 he built a new sixteen-sided barn on the

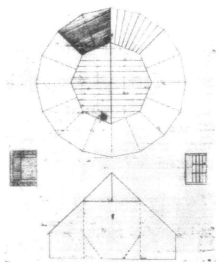

Part of Washington's Plan for His Sixteen-Sided Barn.

Dogue Run Farm. The plan of this barn, drawn by Washington himself, is still preserved and is reproduced herewith. He calculated that one hundred and forty thousand bricks would be required for it and these were made and burnt upon the estate. The barn was particularly notable for a threshing floor thirty feet square, with interstices one and a half inches wide left between the floor boards so that the grain when trodden out by horses or beat out with flails would fall through to the floor below, leaving the straw above.

This floor was to furnish an illustration of what Washington called "the almost impossibility of putting the overseers of this country out of the track they have been accustomed to walk in. I have one of the most convenient barns in this or perhaps any other country, where thirty hands may with great ease be employed in threshing. Half the wheat of the farm was actually stowed in this barn in the straw by my order, for threshing; notwithstanding, when I came home about the middle of September, I found a treading yard not thirty feet from the barn-door, the wheat again brought out of the barn, and horses treading it out in an open exposure, liable to the vicissitudes of the weather."

I think we may safely conclude that this was one of those rare occasions when George lost his temper and "went up in the air!"

Under any conditions treading or flailing out wheat was a slow and unsatisfactory process and, as Washington grew great quantities of this grain, he was alert for a better method. We know that he made inquiries of Arthur Young concerning a threshing machine invented by a certain Winlaw and pictured and described in volume six of the *Annals*, and in 1790 he watched the operation of Baron Poelnitz's mill on the Winlaw model near New York City. This mill was operated by two men and was capable of threshing about two bushels of wheat per hour—pretty slow work as compared with that of a modern thresher. And the grain had to be winnowed, or passed through a fan afterward to separate it from the chaff.

Finally in 1797 he erected a machine on plans evolved by William Booker, who came to Mount Vernon and oversaw the construction. Next April he wrote to Booker that the machine "has by no means answered your expectations or mine," At first it threshed not quite fifty bushels per day, then fell to less than twenty-five, and ultimately got out of order before five hundred bushels had been threshed, though it had used up two bands costing between eight and ten pounds. Booker replied that he had now greatly improved his invention and would come to Mount Vernon and make these additions, but whether or not he ever did so I have failed to discover.

By 1793 the burden of the estate had become so heavy that Washington decided to rent all of it except the Mansion House Farm and accordingly he wrote to Arthur Young telling his desire in the hope that Englishmen might be found to take it over. One man, Parkinson, of whom more hereafter, came to America and looked at one of the farms, but decided not to rent it. Washington's elaborate description of his land in his letter to Young, with an accompanying map, forms one of our best sources of information regarding Mount Vernon, so that we may be grateful that he had the intention even though nothing came of it. The whole of Mount Vernon continued to be cultivated as before until the last year of his life when he rented Dogue Run Farm to his nephew, Lawrence Lewis.

As a public man he was anxious to improve the general state of American agriculture and in his last annual message to Congress recommended the establishment of a board of agriculture to collect and diffuse information and "by premiums and small pecuniary aids to encourage and assist a spirit of discovery and improvement." In this recommendation the example of the English Board of Agriculture and the influence of his friend Arthur Young are discernible. It would have been well for the country if Congress had heeded the advice, but public opinion was not then educated to the need of such a step and almost a century passed before anything of much importance was done by the national government to improve the state of American agriculture.

In farming as in politics Washington was no standpatter. Notwithstanding many discouragements, he could not be kept from trying new things, and he furnished his farms with every kind of improved tool and implement calculated to do better work. At his death he owned not only threshing machines and a Dutch fan, but a wheat drill, a corn drill, a machine for gathering clover seed and another for raking up wheat. Yet most of his countrymen remained content to drop corn by hand, to broadcast their wheat, to tread out their grain and otherwise to follow methods as old as the days of Abel for at least another half century.

He was the first American conservationist. He realized that man owes a duty to the future just as he owes a debt to the past. He deplored the already developing policy of robber exploitation by which our soil and forests have been despoiled, for he foresaw the bitter fruits which such a policy must produce, and indeed was already producing on the fields of Virginia. He was no misanthropic cynic to exclaim, "What has posterity ever done for us that we should concern ourselves for posterity?" His care for the lands of Mount Vernon was evidence of the God-given trait imbedded in the best of men to transmit unimpaired to future generations what has been handed down to them.

His agricultural career has its lessons for us, even though we should not do well to follow some of his methods. The lessons lie rather in his conception of farming as an honorable occupation capable of being put on a better and more scientific basis by the application of brains and intelligence; in his open-minded and progressive seeking after better ways. Many of his experiments failed, it is true, but for his time he was a great Farmer, just as he was a great Patriot, Soldier and Statesman. Patient, hard-working, methodical, willing to sacrifice his own interests to those of the general good, he was one of those men who have helped raise mankind from the level of the brute and his whole career reflects credit upon human nature.

Peace hath its victories no less renowned than war, and the picture of the American Cincinnatus striving as earnestly on the green fields of Mount Vernon as he did upon the scarlet ones of Monmouth and Brandywine, is one that the world can not afford to forget.

CHAPTER IX

THE STOCKMAN

A various times in his career Washington raised deer, turkeys, hogs, cattle, geese, negroes and various other forms of live stock, but his greatest interest seems to have been reserved for horses, sheep and mules.

From his diaries and other papers that have come down to us it is easy to see that during his early married life he paid most attention to his horses. In 1760 he kept a stallion both for his own mares and for those of his neighbors, and we find many entries concerning the animal. Successors were "Leonidas," "Samson," "Steady," "Traveller" and "Magnolia," the last a full-blooded Arabian and probably the finest beast he ever owned. When away from home Washington now and then directed the manager to advertise the animal then reigning or to exhibit him in public places such as fairs. Mares brought to the stallion were kept upon pasture, and foal was guaranteed. Many times the General complained of the difficulty of collecting fees.

During the Revolution he bought twenty-seven worn-out army mares for breeding purposes and soon after he became President he purchased at Lancaster, Pennsylvania, thirteen fine animals for the same use. These last cost him a total of £317.17.6, the price of the highest being £25.7.6 and of the cheapest £22.10. These mares were unusually good animals, as an ordinary beast would have cost only five or six pounds.

In November, 1785, he had on his various Mount Vernon farms a total of one hundred thirty horses, including the Arabian already mentioned. Among the twenty-one animals kept at the Mansion House were his old war horses "Nelson" and "Blewskin," who after bearing their master through the smoke and dangers of many battles lived in peace to a ripe old age on the green fields of Virginia.

In his last days he bought two of the easy-gaited animals known as Narragansetts, a breed, some readers will recall, described at some length by Cooper in *The Last of the Mohicans*. A peculiarity of these beasts was that they moved both legs on a side forward at the same time, that is, they were pacers. Washington's two proved somewhat skittish, and one of them was responsible for the only fall from horseback that we have any record of his receiving. In company with Major Lewis, Mr. Peake, young George

Washington Custis and a groom he was returning in the evening from Alexandria and dismounted for a few moments near a fire on the roadside. When he attempted to mount again the horse sprang forward suddenly and threw him. The others jumped from their horses to assist him, but the old man got up quickly, brushed his clothes and explained that he had been thrown only because he had not yet got seated. All the horses meanwhile had run away and the party started to walk four miles home, but luckily some negroes along the road caught the fugitives and brought them back. Washington insisted upon mounting his animal again and rode home without further incident. This episode happened only a few weeks before his death.

Like every farmer he found that his horses had a way of growing old. Those with which he had personal associations, like "Blueskin" and "Nelson," he kept until they died of old age. With others he sometimes followed a different course. In 1792 we find his manager, Whiting, writing: "We have several Old Horses that are not worth keeping thro winter. One at Ferry has not done one days work these 18 Months. 2 at Muddy hole one a horse with the Pole evil which I think will not get well the other an Old Mare was not capable of work last summer. Likewise the Horse called old Chatham and the Lame Horse that used to go in the Waggon now in a one horse Cart. If any thing could be Got for them it might be well but they are not worth keeping after Christmas." No doubt a sentimental person would say that Washington ought to have kept these old servants, but he had many other superannuated servants of the human kind upon his hands, so he replied that Whiting might dispose of the old horses "as you judge best for my interest."

Now and then his horses met with accidents. Thus on February 22, 1760, his horse "Jolly" got his right foreleg "mashed to pieces," probably by a falling limb. "Did it up as well as I could this night." "Saturday, Feb. 23d. Had the Horse Slung upon Canvas and his leg fresh set, following Markleham's directions as well as I could." Two days later the horse fell out of the sling and hurt himself so badly that he had to be killed.

Of Washington's skill as a trainer of horses his friend De Chastellux writes thus: "The weather being fair, on the 26th, I got on horseback, after breakfasting with the general—he was so attentive as to give me the horse he rode, the day of my arrival, which I had greatly commended—I found him as good as he is handsome; but above all, perfectly well broke, and well trained, having a good mouth, easy in hand, and stopping short in a gallop without bearing the bit—I mention these minute particulars, because it is the general himself who breaks all his own horses; and he is a very excellent and bold horseman, leaping the highest fences, and going extremely quick, without standing upon his stirrups, bearing on the bridle, or letting his horse run wild,

—circumstances which young men look upon as so essential a part of English horsemanship, that they would rather break a leg or an arm than renounce them."

Comparatively few farmers in Virginia kept sheep, yet as early as 1758 Washington's overseer at Mount Vernon reported sixty-five old sheep and forty-eight lambs; seven years later the total number was one hundred fifty-six. The next year he records that he "put my English Ram Lamb to 65 Ewes," so that evidently he was trying to improve the breed. What variety this ram belonged to he does not say. Near the end of his career he had some of Bakewell's breed, an English variety that put on fat rapidly and hence were particularly desirable for mutton.

During his long absences from home his sheep suffered grievously, for sheep require a skilled care that few of his managers or overseers knew how to give. But sheep were an important feature of the English agriculture that he imitated, and he persisted in keeping them. In 1793 he had over six hundred.

"Before I left home in the spring of 1789," he wrote to Arthur Young, "I had improved that species of my stock so much as to get 5-1/4 lbs of Wool as the average of the fleeces of my whole flock,—and at the last shearing they did not yield me 2-1/2 lbs.—By procuring (if I am able) good rams and giving the necessary attention, I hope to get them up again for they are with me, as you have declared them to be with you, that part of my stock in which I most delight."

In 1789, by request, he sent Young "a fleece of a midling size and quality." Young had this made up into cloth and returned it to the General.

In 1793 we find our Farmer giving such instructions to Whiting as to cull out the unthrifty sheep and transform them into mutton and to choose a few of the best young males to keep as rams. Whiting, however, did not manage the flock well, for the following February we find Pearce, the new manager, writing:

"I am sorry to have to inform you that the stock of sheep at Both Union and Dogue Run farms are Some of them Dicing Every Week—& a great many of Them will be lost, let what will be done—Since I came I have had shelters made for them & Troughs to feed them In & to give them salt—& have attended to them myself & was In hopes to have saved those that I found to be weak, but they were too far gone—and Several of the young Cattle at Dogue Run was past all Recovery when I come & some have died already & several more I am afraid must die before spring, they are so very poor and weak."

Washington, according to his own account, was the first American to attempt the raising of mules. Soon after the Revolution he asked our representative in

Spain to ascertain whether it would be possible "to procure permission to extract a Jack ass of the best breed." At that time the exportation of these animals from Spain was forbidden by law, but Florida Blanca, the Spanish minister of state, brought the matter to the attention of the king, who in a fit of generosity proceeded to send the American hero two jacks and two jennets. One of the jacks died on the way over, but the other animals, in charge of a Spanish caretaker, reached Boston, and Washington despatched an overseer to escort them to Mount Vernon, where they arrived on the fifth of December, 1785. An interpreter named Captain Sullivan was brought down from Alexandria, and through him the General propounded to the caretaker many grave inquiries regarding the care of the beasts, the answers being carefully set down in writing.

"Royal Gift," as he was duly christened, probably by the negro groom, Peter, who seems to have considered it beneath his dignity to minister to any but royalty, was a large animal. According to careful measurements taken on the porch at Mount Vernon he was fifteen hands high, and his body and limbs were very large in proportion to his height; his ears were fourteen inches long, and his vocal cords were good. He was, however, a sluggish beast, and the sea voyage had affected him so unfavorably that for some time he was of little use. In letters to Lafayette and others Washington commented facetiously upon the beast's failure to appreciate "republican

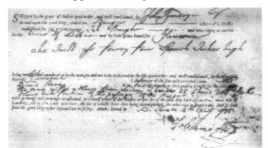

Bill of Lading for "Royal Gift".

enjoyment." Ultimately, however, "Royal Gift" recovered his strength and ambition and proved a valuable piece of property. He was presently sent on a lour of the South, and while in South Carolina was in the charge of Colonel William Washington, a hero of the Cowpens and many other battles. The profits from the tour amounted to $678.64, yet poor "Royal Gift" seems to have experienced some rough usage on the way thither, arriving lame and thin and in a generally debilitated condition. The General wrote to the Colonel about it thus:

"From accounts which I have received from some gentlemen in Virginia he was most abominably treated on the journey by the man to whom he was entrusted;—for, instead of moving him slowly and steadily along as he ought, he was prancing (with the Jack) from one public meeting or place to another in a gate which could not but prove injurious to an animal who had hardly ever been out of a walk before—and afterward, I presume, (in order to recover lost time) rushed him beyond what he was able to bear the remainder of the journey."

No doubt the beast aroused great curiosity along the way among people who had never before set eyes upon such a creature. We can well believe that the cry, "General Washington's jackass is coming!" was always sufficient to attract a gaping crowd. And many would be the sage comments upon the animal's voice and appearance.

In 1786 Lafayette sent Washington from the island of Malta another jack and two jennets, besides some Chinese pheasants and partridges. The animals landed at Baltimore in November and reached Mount Vernon in good condition later in the month. To Campion, the man who accompanied them, Washington gave "30 Louis dores for his trouble." The new jack, the "Knight of Malta," as he was called, was a smaller beast than "Royal Gift," and his ears measured only twelve inches, but he was well formed and had the ferocity of a tiger.

By crossing the two strains Washington ultimately obtained a jack called "Compound," who united in his person the size and strength of the "Gift" with the courage and activity of the "Knight." The General also raised many mules, which he found to be good workers and more cheaply kept in condition than horses.

Henceforward the peaceful quiet of Mount Vernon was broken many times a day by sounds which, if not musical or mellifluous, were at least jubilant and joyous.

Evidently the sounds in no way disturbed the General, for in 1788 we find him describing the acquisitions in enthusiastic terms to Arthur Young. He called the mules "a very excellent race of animals," cheap to keep and willing workers. Recalling, perhaps, that a king's son once rode upon a mule, he proposes to breed heavy ones from "Royal Gift" for draft purposes and lighter ones from the "Knight" for saddle or carriage. He adds: "Indeed in a few years, I intend to drive no other in my carriage, having appropriated for the sole purpose of breeding them, upwards of twenty of my best mares."

Ah, friend George, what would the world not give to see thee and thy wife Martha driving in the Mount Vernon coach down Pennsylvania Avenue behind four such long-eared beasts!

In all his stock raising, as in most other matters, Washington was greatly hampered by the carelessness of his overseers and slaves. It is notorious that free negroes will often forget or fail to water and feed their own horses, and it may easily be believed that when not influenced by fear, slaves would neglect the stock of their master. Among the General's papers I have found a list of the animals that died upon his Mount Vernon estate from April 16, 1789, to December 25, 1790. In that period of about twenty months he lost thirty-three horses, thirty-two cattle and sixty-five sheep! Considering the number of stock he had, a fifth of that loss would have been excessive. During most of the period he was away from home looking after the affairs of the nation and in his absence his own affairs suffered.

Hardly a report of his manager did not contain some bad news. Thus one of January, 1791, states that "the Young black Brood Mare, with a long tail, which Came from Pennsylvania, said to be four Years old next spring ... was found with her thigh broke quite in two." This happened on the Mansion House farm. On another farm a sheep was reported to have been killed by dogs while a second had died suddenly, perhaps from eating some poisonous plant.

Dogs, in fact, constituted an ever present menace to the sheep and it was only by constant watchfulness that the owner kept his negroes from overrunning the place with worthless curs. In 1792 he wrote to his manager: "I not only approve of your killing those Dogs which have been the occasion of the late loss, & of thinning the Plantations of others, but give it as a positive order that after saying what dog, or dogs shall remain, if any negro presumes under any pretence whatsoever, to preserve, or bring one into the family, that he shall be severely punished, and the dog hanged.—I was obliged to adopt this practice whilst I resided at home, and from the same motive, that is for the preservation of my Sheep and Hogs.... It is not for any good purpose Negroes raise, and keep dogs; but to aid them in their night robberies; for it is astonishing to see the command under which the dogs are."

After the Revolution, in imitation of English farmers, he made use of hurdles in pasturing sheep and milk cows. Thereby he secured more even distribution of the manure, which was one of his main objects in raising stock.

Washington's interest in cattle seems to have been less intense than was the case with some other kinds of stock. He always had a great number of cows, bulls, oxen and calves upon his farms—in 1793 over three hundred "black cattle" of all sorts. He was accustomed to brand his cattle with the letters "G.W.," the location of the brand on the body indicating the farm on which the beast was raised. To what extent he endeavored to improve the breed of his cattle I am unable to say, but I have found that as early as 1770 he owned an English bull, which in July he killed and sold to the crew of the British frigate *Boston*, which lay in the Potomac off his estate. In 1797 he made inquiries looking toward the purchase of an improved bull calf from a cattle breeder named Gough, but upon learning that the price was two hundred dollars he decided not to invest. Gough, however, heard of Washington's interest in his animals, and being an admirer of the General, gave him a calf. An English farmer, Parkinson, who saw the animal in 1798, describes him in terms the reverse of enthusiastic, and of this more hereafter.

A large part of the heavy work on all the farms was done by oxen. In November, 1785, there were thirteen yoke of these beasts on the Mount Vernon estate and the number was sometimes still larger. In 1786 Washington recorded putting "a Collar on a large Bull in order to break him to the draft.— at first he was sulky and restive but came to by degrees." The owner always aimed to have enough oxen broken so that none would have to be worked too hard, but he did not always succeed in his aim. When they attained the age of eight years the oxen were usually fattened and killed for beef.

The management of the milk cows seems to have been very poor. In May, 1793, we find the absent owner writing to his manager: "If for the sake of making a little butter (for which I shall get scarcely anything) my calves are starved, & die, it may be compared to stopping the spigot, and opening the faucit." Evidently the making of butter was almost totally discontinued, for in his last instructions, completed only a few days before his death, he wrote: "And It is hoped and will be expected, that more effectual measures will be pursued to make butter another year; for it is almost beyond belief, that from 101 Cows actually reported on a late enumeration of the Cattle, that I am obliged to *buy butter* for the use of my family."

In his later years he became somewhat interested in the best methods of feeding cattle and once suggested that the experiment be tried of fattening one bullock on potatoes, another on corn, and a third on a mixture of both, "keeping an exact account of the time they are fatting, and what is eaten of each, and of hay, by the different steers; that a judgment may be formed of the best and least expensive mode of stall feeding beef for market, or for my own use."

During his early farming operations his swine probably differed little if at all from the razor-backs of his neighbors. They ranged half wild in the woods in summer and he once expressed the opinion that fully half the pigs raised were stolen by the slaves, who loved roast pork fully as well as did their master. In the fall the shoats were shut up to fatten. More than a hundred were required each year to furnish meat for the people on the estate; the average weight was usually less than one hundred forty pounds. Farmers in the Middle West would to-day have their Poland Chinas or Durocs of the same age weighing two hundred fifty to three hundred pounds. Still the smallness of Washington's animals does not necessarily indicate such bad management as may at first glance appear. Until of considerable size the pigs practically made their own living, eating roots and mast in the woods, and they did not require much grain except during fattening time. And, after all, as the story has it, "what's time to a hawg?"

In his later years he seems to have taken more interest in his pigs. By 1786 he had decided that when fattening they ought to be put into closed pens with a plank floor, a roof, running water and good troughs. A visitor to Mount Vernon in 1798 says that he had "about 150 of the Guinea kind, with short legs and hollow back," so it is evident that he was experimenting with new breeds. These Guinea swine were red in color, and it is said that the breed was brought to America from west Africa by slave traders. It was to these animals that Washington fed the by-products of his distillery.

In the slaughtering of animals he tried experiments as he did in so many other matters. In 1768 he killed a wether sheep which weighed one hundred three pounds gross. He found that it made sixty pounds of meat worth three pence per pound, five and a half of tallow at seven and a half pence, three of wool at fifteen pence, and the skin was worth one shilling and three pence, a total of £1.3.5. One object of such experiments was to ascertain whether it was more profitable to butcher animals or sell them on the hoof.

Washington also raised chickens, turkeys, swans, ducks, geese and various other birds and beasts. In 1788 Gouverneur Morris sent him two Chinese pigs and with them "a pair of Chinese geese, which are really the foolishest geese I ever beheld; for they choose all times for setting but in the spring, and one of them is even now [November] actually engaged in that business." Of some golden pheasants that had been brought from China the General said that before seeing the birds he had considered that pictures of them must be "only works of fancy, but now I find them to be only Portraits."

The fact is that his friends and admirers sent him so many feathered or furred creatures that toward the end of his life he was the proprietor of a considerable zoo.

Notwithstanding mismanagement by his employees and slaves, Washington accumulated much valuable domestic stock. In his will, made the year of his death, he lists the following: "1 Covering horse, 5 Cob. horses—4 Riding do —Six brood mares—20 working horses and mares,—2 Covering jacks & 3 young ones 10 she asses—42 working mules—15 younger ones. 329 head of horned cattle. 640 head of Sheep, and the large stock of hogs, the precise number unknown." He further states that his manager believes the stock worth seven thousand pounds, but he conservatively sets it down at fifteen thousand six hundred fifty-three dollars.

———————————————

CHAPTER X

THE HORTICULTURIST AND LANDSCAPE GARDENER

Washington's work as a horticulturist prior to the educating influences of the Revolution was mostly utilitarian. That he had a peach orchard as early as 1760 is proven by an entry in his diary for February 22: "Laid in part, the Worm of a fence round the Peach orchard." Just where this orchard stood I am not quite certain, but it was probably on the slope near the old tomb.

He learned how to propagate and "wed" his own trees and in 1763 was particularly active. On March 21st he recorded that he had "Grafted 40 cherries, viz 12 Bullock Hearts, 18 very fine May Cherry, 10 Coronation. Also grafted 12 Magnum Bonum Plums. Also planted 4 Nuts of the Mediterranean Pame in the Pen where the Chestnut grows—sticks by East. Note, the Cherrys and Plums came from Collo. Masons Nuts from Mr. Gr[een's.] Set out 55 cuttings of the Madeira Grape."

A little later he grafted quinces on pear and apple stocks; also he grafted "Spanish pairs," "Butter pears," "Bergamy Pears," "Newtown Pippins," "43 of the Maryland Red Strick," etc., and transplanted thirty-five young crab scions. These scions he obtained by planting the pumice of wild crab apples from which cider had been made. They were supposed to make hardier stocks than those grown from ordinary seeds.

He grafted many cherries, plums, etc., in March, 1764, and yet again in the spring of 1765, when he put English mulberry scions on wild mulberry stocks. In that year "Peter Green came to me a Gardener." In 1768 and 1771 he planted grapes in the inclosure below the vegetable garden and in March, 1775, he again grafted cherries and also planted peach seeds and seeds of the "Mississippi nut" or pecan.

Long before this he had begun to gather fruits from his early trees and vines. Being untroubled by San Jose scale and many other pests that now make life miserable to the fruit grower, he grew fine products and no doubt enjoyed them.

His esthetic sense was not yet fully developed, but he was always desirous of having his possessions make a good appearance, and by 1768 was beginning to think of beautifying his grounds. In that year he expressed a wish that he later carried out, namely to have about his mansion house every possible specimen of native tree or shrub noted for beauty of form, leaf or flower.

Even amid the trials of the Revolution this desire was not forgotten. In 1782 he directed Lund Washington, his manager, to plant locusts and other ornamental trees and shrubs at the ends of the house. He wrote that such trees would be more likely to live if taken from the open fields than from the woods because the change of environment would be less pronounced. To what extent the work was carried I have been unable to ascertain, for, as elsewhere stated, very little of his correspondence with his manager during these years survives.

He returned from the Revolution with a strong desire to beautify his estate, a desire in part due no doubt to seeing beautiful homes elsewhere and to contact with cultured people, both Americans and foreigners. One of his first tasks was to rebuild and enlarge his house. From a small house of eight rooms he transformed Mount Vernon into the present large mansion, ninety-six feet and four inches long by thirty-two feet in depth, with two floors and an attic, an immense cellar and the magnificent portico overlooking the Potomac. The plans and specifications he drew with his own hands, and those who have visited the place will hardly deny that the mansion fits well into its setting and that, architects tell us, is a prime consideration. The flagstones for the floor of the portico he imported from Whitehaven, England, and these still remain in place, though many are cracked or broken.

The portico runs the entire length of the house, is over fourteen feet deep and its floor is one hundred twenty-four feet ten and one-half inches above high water-mark, according to calculations made by Washington himself. From it one commands miles of the Potomac and of the Maryland shore and there are few such noble prospects in America. Washington owned a telescope and spy glasses and with them could watch the movements of ships and boats on the river. The portico was a sort of trysting place for the family and visitors on summer afternoons and evenings, and some of the thirty or so Windsor chairs bought for it are still in existence.

This was the second time our Farmer reconstructed his house, as in 1758-60 he had made numerous

West Front of Mansion House, Showing Bowling Green and Part of Serpentine Drive.

Experimental Plot, with Servants' Quarters (restored) in Background.

alterations[6]. In 1758 he paid John Patterson £328.0.5 for work done upon it, and the whole house was pretty thoroughly renovated and remodeled in preparation for the reception of a new mistress. In March, 1760, we find the owner contracting with William Triplett "to build me two houses in front of my house (plastering them also) and running walls to them from the great house and from the great house to the washouse and kitchen also." By the "front" he means the west front, as that part toward the river is really the rear of the mansion. Hitherto the house had stood detached and these walls were the originals of the colonnades, still a noticeable feature of the building.

[6] In 1775 a Frenchman was engaged to panel the main hall and apply stucco ornaments to the ceilings of the parlor and dining-room.

Owing to the absence of a diary of his home activities during 1784 we can not trace in detail his work that year upon either his house or grounds, but we know such facts as that he was ordering materials for the house and that he had his French friend Malesherbes and others collecting vines and plants for him.

With January 1, 1785, he began a new diary, and from it we ascertain that on the twelfth, on a ride about his estate, he observed many trees and shrubs suitable for transplanting. Thereafter he rarely rode out without noticing some crab, holly, magnolia, pine or other young tree that would serve his purpose. He was more alive to the beauties of nature than he had once been, or at least more inclined to comment upon them. On an April day he notes that "the flower of the Sassafras was fully out and looked well—an intermixture of this and Red bud I conceive would look very pretty—the latter crowned with the former or vice versa." He was no gushing spring poet, but when the sap was running, the flowers blooming and the birds singing he felt it all in his heart—perhaps more deeply than do some who say more about it.

On January 19th of this year he began laying out his grounds on a new plan. This plan, as completed, provided for sunken walls or "Haw has!" at the ends of the mansion, and on the west front a large elliptical lawn or bowling green such as still exists there. Along the sides of the lawn he laid out a serpentine drive or carriage way, to be bordered with a great variety of shade trees on each side and a "Wilderness" on the outside. At the extreme west, where the entrance stood, the trees were omitted so that from the house one could see down a long vista, cut through the oaks and evergreens, the lodge gate three-quarters of a mile away. On each side of the opening in the lawn stood a small artificial mound, and just in front of the house a sun-dial by which each day, when the weather was clear, he set his watch. A sun-dial stands on the same spot now but, alas, it is not the original. That was given away or sold by one of the subsequent owners.

This same spring our Farmer records planting ivy, limes and lindens sent by his good friend Governor Clinton of New York; lilacs, mock oranges, aspen, mulberries, black gums, berried thorns, locusts, sassafras, magnolia, crabs, service berries, catalpas, papaws, honey locusts, a live oak from Norfolk, yews, aspens, swamp berries, hemlocks, twelve horse chestnut sent by "Light Horse Harry" Lee, twelve cuttings of tree box, buckeye nuts brought by him the preceding year from the mouth of Cheat River, eight nuts from a tree called "the Kentucke Coffee tree," a row of shell bark hickory nuts from New York, some filberts from "sister Lewis." His brother John sent him four barrels of holly seeds, which he sowed in the semicircle north of the front gate; in the south semicircle, from the kitchen to the south "Haw ha!"; and from the servants' hall to the north "Haw ha!"

Nor did he neglect more utilitarian work, for in April he grafted many cherries, pears and other fruit trees. Such work was continued at intervals till his death.

In raising fruit, as in many other things, he was troubled by the thieving propensities of the slaves. September tenth of this year he records that because of the scarcity of apples and the depredations that were being committed "every Night upon the few I have, I found it necessary (tho much too early) to gather and put them up for Winter use."

The spring of 1785 proved an exceptionally dry one and he was forced to be absent from home several days, leaving the care of the trees and shrubs to his careless lazy servants. He records that they *said* that they watered them according to directions, but he seems to doubt it. At all events, "Most of my transplanted trees have a sickly look.—The small Pines in the Wilderness are entirely dead.—The larger ones in the Walks, for the most part appear to be alive (as yet)—almost the whole of the Holly are dead—many of the Ivy, wch. before looked healthy & well seem to be declining—few of the Crab trees had put forth leaves; not a single Ash tree has unfolded its buds; whether owing to the trees declining or any other cause, I know not.... The lime trees, which had some appearance of Budding when I went away, are now withering —and the Horse chestnut & Tree box from Colo. Harry Lee's discover little signs of shooting.—the Hemlock is almost entirely dead, & bereft of their leaves;—and so are the live Oak.—In short half the Trees in the Shrubberies & many in the Walk are dead & declin[in]g."

Nevertheless he refused to be discouraged and proceeded to plant forty-eight mahogany tree seeds brought by his nephew, George A. Washington, from the West Indies. He also set out a "Palmetto Royal" in the garden and sowed or planted sandbox trees, palmettos, physic nuts, pride of Chinas, live oaks, accacias, bird peppers, "Caya pepper," privet, guinea grass, and a great variety of Chinese grasses, the names of which, such as *"In che fa," "all san fa" "se lon fa,"* he gravely set down in his diary.

The dry weather continued and presently he notes that all the poplars, black gums and pines, most of the mulberries, all of the crab apples and papaws, most of the hemlock and sassafras, and several of the cedars are dead, while the tops of the live oaks are dead but shoots are coming up from the trunks and roots. The Chinese grasses are in a bad way, and those that have come up are almost entirely destroyed either by insects or drought. None of this grass survived the winter, though he took the trouble to cover it with straw.

During the fall of 1785 and spring of 1786 he sowed the lawn with English grass seeds, replaced the dead trees in the serpentine walks and shrubberies, and sent two hundred and fifteen apple trees to his River Plantation. He made the two low mounds already mentioned and planted thereon weeping willows. He set out stocks of imported hawthorns, four yellow jessamines, twenty-five of the Palinurus for hedges, forty-six pistacia nuts and seventy-five pyramidical cypress, which last were brought to him by the botanist Michaux from the King of France. As 1786 was one of the wettest summers ever known, his plants and trees lived better than they had done the preceding year.

During this period and until the end of his life he was constantly receiving trees and shrubs from various parts of the world. Thus in 1794 he sent to Alexandria by Thomas Jefferson a bundle of "Poccon [pecan] or Illinois nut," which in some way had come to him at Philadelphia. He instructed the gardener to set these out at Mount Vernon, also to sow some seeds of the East India hemp that had been left in his care. The same year thirty-nine varieties of tropical plants, including the bread fruit tree, came to him from a well wisher in Jamaica. At other times he sowed seeds of the cucumber tree, chickory and "colliflower" and planted ivy and wild honeysuckle. Again he once more planted pecans and hickory nuts. It can hardly be that at his advanced age he expected to derive any personal good from either of these trees, but he was very fond of nuts, eating great quantities for dessert, and the liking inclined him to grow trees that produced them. In this, as in many other matters, he planted for the benefit of posterity.

In order to care for his exotic plants he built adjoining the upper garden a considerable conservatory or hothouse. In this he placed many of the plants sent to him as presents and also purchased many others from the collection of the celebrated botanist, John Bartram, at Philadelphia. The structure, together with the servants' quarters adjoining, was burned down in December, 1835, and when the historian Lossing visited Mount Vernon in 1858 nothing remained of these buildings except bare walls crumbling to decay. Of the movable plants that had belonged to Washington there remained in 1858 only a lemon tree, a century plant and a sago palm, all of which have since died. The conservatory and servants' quarters have, however, been rebuilt and the conservatory restocked with plants such as Washington kept in it. The buildings probably look much as they did in his time.

One of the sights to-day at Mount Vernon is the formal garden, which all who have visited the place will remember. Strangely enough it seems impossible to discover exactly when this was laid out as it now stands. The guides follow tradition and tell visitors that Washington set out the box hedge, the principal feature, after his marriage, and that he told Martha that she should be mistress of this flower garden and he the master of the vegetable garden. It is barely possible that he did set out the hedges at that time, but, if so, it must have been in 1759, for no mention is made of it in the diary begun in 1760. In April, 1785, we find by his diary that he planted twelve cuttings of the "tree box" and again in the spring of 1787 he planted in his shrubberies some holly trees, "also … some of the slips of the tree box." But of box hedges I can find no mention in any of the papers I have seen. One guess is about as good as another, and I am inclined to believe that if they were planted in his time, it was done during his presidency by one of his gardeners, perhaps Butler or the German, Ehler. They may have been set out long after his death. At all events the garden was modeled after the formal gardens of Europe and the idea was not original with him.

East of the formal garden lies a plot of ground that he used for agricultural experiments. The vegetable garden was south of the Bowling Green and separated from it by a brick wall. Here utility was lord and a great profusion of products was raised for the table. Washington took an interest in its management and I have found an entry in his diary recording the day that green peas were available for the first time that year. Evidently he was fond of them.

The bent of our Farmer's mind was to the practical, yet he took pride in the appearance of his estate. "I shall begrudge no reasonable expense that will contribute to the improvement and neatness of my farms," he wrote one of his managers, "for nothing pleases me better than to see them in good order, and everything trim, handsome, and thriving about them; nor nothing hurts me more than to find them otherwise."

Live hedges tend to make a place look well and it was probably this and his passion for trees that caused Washington to go in extensively for hedges about his farms. They took the place of wooden fences and saved trees and also grew more trees and bushes. His ordinary course in building a fence was to have a trench dug on each side of the line and the dirt thrown toward the center. Upon the ridge thus formed he built a post and rail fence and along it planted cedars, locusts, pines, briars or thorn bushes to discourage cattle and other stock. The trenches not only increased the efficiency of the fence but also served as ditches. In many places they are still discernible. The lines of the hedges are also often marked in many places by trees which, though few or none can be the originals, are descended from the roots or seeds of those trees. Cedar and locust trees are particularly noticeable.

First page of the Diary for 1760.

In 1794 our Farmer had five thousand white thorn sent from England for hedge purposes, but they arrived late in the spring and few survived and even these did not thrive very well. Another time he sent from Philadelphia two bushels of honey locust seed to be planted in his nursery. These are only instances of his activities in this direction.

Much of what he undertook as a planter of trees failed for one reason or another, most of all because he attended to the business of his country at the expense of his own, but much that he attempted succeeded and enough still remains to enable us to realize that by his efforts he made his estate attractive. He was no Barbarian or Philistine. He had a sense of beauty and it is only in recent years that his countrymen, absorbed in material undertakings, have begun to appreciate the things that he was enjoying so long ago.

"The visitor at Mount Vernon still finds a charm no art alone could give, in trees from various climes, each a witness of the taste that sought, or the love that sent them, in fields which the desolating step of war reverently passed by, in flowers whose root is not in graves, yet tinged with the lifeblood of the heart that cherished them from childhood to old age. On those acres we move beneath the shade or shelter of the invisible tree which put forth whatever meets the eye, and has left some sign on each object, large or small. Still planted beside his river, he brings forth fruit in his season. Nor does his leaf wither."

CHAPTER XI

WHITE SERVANTS AND OVERSEERS

In colonial Virginia, as in most other new countries, one of the greatest problems that confronted the settlers was that of labor. It took human muscle to clear away the forest and tend the crops, and the quantity of human muscle available was small. One solution of the problem was the importation of black slaves, and of this solution as it concerned Washington something will be said in a separate chapter. Another solution was the white indentured servant.

Some of these white servants were political offenders, such as the followers of Monmouth, who were punished by transportation for a term of years or for life to the plantations. Others were criminals or unfortunate debtors who were sold in America instead of being sent to jail. Others were persons who had been kidnapped and carried across the sea into servitude. Yet others were men and women who voluntarily bound themselves to work for a term of years in payment of their passage to the colonies. By far the largest number of the white servants in Washington's day belonged to this last-mentioned class, who were often called "redemptioners." Some of these were ambitious, well-meaning people, perhaps skilled artisans, who after working out their time became good citizens and often prospered. A few were even well educated. In favor of the convicts, however, little could be said. In general they were ignorant and immoral and greatly lowered the level of the population in the Southern States, the section to which most of them were sent.

Whether they came to America of their own free will or not such servants were subjected to stringent regulations and were compelled to complete their terms of service. If they ran away, they could be pursued and brought back by force, and the papers of the day were full of advertisements for such absconders. Owing to their color and the ease with which they found sympathizers among the white population, however, the runaways often managed to make good their escape.

To give a complete list of Washington's indentured servants, even if it were possible, would be tedious and tiresome. For the most part he bought them in order to obtain skilled workmen. Thus in 1760 we find him writing to a Doctor Ross, of Philadelphia, to purchase for him a joiner, a brick-layer and a gardener, if any ship with servants was in port. As late as 1786 he bought the time of a Dutchman named Overdursh, who was a ditcher and mower, and of his wife, a spinner, washer and milker; also their daughter. The same year he "received from on board the Brig Anna, from Ireland, two servant men for whom I agreed yesterday—viz—Thomas Ryan, a shoemaker, and Cavan Bowen a Tayler Redemptioners for 3 years service by Indenture." These cost him twelve pounds each. The story of his purchase of servants for his western lands is told in another place, as is also that of his plan to import Palatines for the same purpose.

On the day of Lexington and Concord, but before the news of that conflict reached Virginia, two of his indentured servants ran away and he published a lengthy advertisement of them in the Virginia *Gazette*, offering a reward of forty dollars for the return of both or twenty dollars for the return of either. They were described as follows:

"THOMAS SPEARS, a joiner, born in *Bristol*, about 20 years of age, 5 feet 6 inches and a half high, slender made. He has light grey or blueish colored eyes, a little pock-marked, and freckled, with sandy colored hair, cut short; his voice is coarse, and somewhat drawling. He took with him a coat, waistcoat, and breeches, of light brown duffil, with black horn buttons, a light colored cloth waistcoat, old leather breeches, check and oznabrig shirts, a pair of old ribbed ditto, new oznabrig trowsers, and a felt hat, not much the worse for wear. WILLIAM WEBSTER, a brick maker, born in *Scotland*, and talks pretty broad. He is about 5 feet six inches high and well made, rather turned of 30, with light brown hair, and roundish face.... They went off in a small yawl, with turpentine sides and bottom, the inside painted with a mixture of tar and red lead."

In the course of his business career Washington also employed a considerable number of free white men, who likewise were usually skilled workers or overseers. He commonly engaged them for the term of one year and by written contracts, which he drew up himself, a thing he had learned to do when a boy by copying legal forms. Many of these papers still survive and contracts with joiners and gardeners jostle inaugural addresses and opinions of cabinet meetings.

As a rule the hired employees received a house, an allowance of corn, flour, meat and perhaps other articles, the money payment being comparatively small.

Some of the contracts contain peculiar stipulations. That with a certain overseer provided: "And whereas there are a number of whiskey stills very contiguous to the said Plantations, and many idle, drunken and dissolute People continually resorting the same, priding themselves in debauching sober and well-inclined Persons the said Edd. Voilett doth promise as well for his own sake as his employers to avoid them as he ought."

Probably most readers have heard of the famous contract with the gardener Philip Bater, who had a weakness for the output of stills such as those mentioned above. It was executed in 1787 and, in consideration of Bater's agreement "not to be disguised with liquor except on times hereinafter mentioned," provided that he should be given "four dollars at Christmas, with which he may be drunk four days and four nights; two dollars at Easter to effect the same purpose; two dollars at Whitsuntide to be drunk for two days; a dram in the morning, and a drink of grog at dinner at noon."

Washington's most famous white servant was Thomas Bishop, who figures in some books as a negro. He had been the personal servant of General Braddock, and tradition says that the dying General commended him to Washington. At all events Washington took him into his service at ten pounds per year and, except for a short interval about 1760, Bishop remained one of his retainers until death. It was Bishop and John Alton who accompanied Washington on his trip to New York and Boston in 1756—that trip in the course of which, according to imaginative historians, the young officer became enamored of the heiress Mary Phillipse. Doubtless the men made a brave show along the way, for we know that Washington had ordered for them "2 complete livery suits for servants; with a spare cloak and all other necessary trimmings for two suits more. I would have you choose the livery by our arms, only as the field of arms is white, I think the clothes had better not be quite so, but nearly like the inclosed. The trimmings and facings of scarlet, and a scarlet waist coat. If livery lace is not quite disused, I should be glad to have the cloaks laced. I like that fashion best, and two silver laced hats for the above servants."

When the Revolution came Bishop was too old to take the field and was left at home as the manager of a plantation. He was allowed a house, for he had married and was now the father of a daughter. He lived to a great age, but on fair days, when the Farmer was at home, the old man always made it a point to grasp his cane and walk out to the road to see his master ride by, to salute him and to pass a friendly word. He seems to have thought of leaving Mount Vernon with his daughter in 1794, for the President wrote to Pearce: "Old Bishop must be taken care of whether he goes or stays." He died the following January, while Washington was away in Philadelphia.

Custis tells an amusing story of Bishop's daughter Sally. Following the Revolution two of Washington's aides-de-camp, Colonels Smith and Humphreys, the latter a poet of some pretensions, spent considerable time at Mount Vernon arranging the General's military papers. One afternoon Smith strolled out from the Mansion House for relaxation and came upon Sally, then in her teens and old enough to be interesting to a soldier, milking a cow. When she started for the house with the pail of milk the Colonel gallantly stepped forward and asked to be permitted to carry it. But Sally had heard from her father dire tales of what befell damsels who had anything to do with military men and the fact that Smith was a fine-looking young fellow in no way lessened her sense of peril. In great panic she flung down the pail, splashing the contents over the officer, and ran screaming to the house. Smith followed, intent upon allaying her alarm and ran plump into old Bishop, who at once accused him of attempting to philander with the girl, turned a deaf ear to all the Colonel's explanations, and declared that he would bring word of the offense to his honor the General, nay more, to Mrs. Washington!

In great alarm the Colonel betook himself toward the Mansion House pondering upon some way of getting himself out of the scrape he had fallen into. At last he bethought himself of Billy Lee, the mulatto body servant, and these two old soldiers proceeded to hold a council of war. Smith said: "It's bad enough, Billy, for this story to get to the General's ears, but to those of the lady will never do; and then there's Humphreys, he will be out upon me in a d—d long poem that will spread my misfortunes from Dan to Beersheba!" At last it was decided that Billy should act as special ambassador to Bishop and endeavor to divert him from his purpose. Meanwhile Bishop had got out his old clothes—Cumberland cocked hat and all—of the period of the French War, had dressed with great care and, taking up his staff, had laid his line of march straight to the Mansion House. Billy met him midway upon the road and much skirmishing ensued, Billy taking two lines of attack: first, that Smith was a perfect gentleman, and, second, that Bishop had no business to have such a devilishly pretty daughter. Finally these tactics prevailed, Bishop took the right about, and a guinea dropped into the ambassador's palm completed the episode.

In due time Sally lost her dreadful fear of men and married the plantation carpenter, Thomas Green, with whose shiftless ways, described elsewhere, Washington put up for a long time for the sake of "his family." Ultimately Green quitted Washington's service and seems to have deserted his wife or else died; at all events she and her family were left in distressed circumstances. She wrote a letter to Washington begging assistance and he instructed his manager to aid her to the extent of £20 but to tell her that if she set up a shop in Alexandria, as she thought of doing, she must not buy anything of his negroes. He seems to have allowed her a little wood, flour and meat at killing time and in 1796 instructed Pearce that if she and her family were really in distress, as reported, to afford them some relief, "but in my opinion it had better be in anything than money, for I very strongly suspect that all that has, and perhaps all that will be given to her in that article, is applied more in rigging herself, than in the purchase of real and useful necessaries for her family."

By his will Washington left Sally Green and Ann Walker, daughter of John Alton, each one hundred dollars in "consideration of the attachment of their father[s] to me."

Alton entered Washington's service even before Bishop, accompanying him as a body servant on the Braddock campaign and suffering a serious illness. He subsequently was promoted to the management of a plantation and enjoyed Washington's confidence and esteem. It was with a sad heart that Washington penned in his diary for 1785: "Last night Jno. Alton an Overseer of mine in the Neck—an old & faithful Servant who has lived with me 30 odd years died—and this evening the wife of Thos. Bishop, another old Servant who had lived with me an equal number of years also died."

The adoption of Mrs. Washington's two youngest grandchildren, Nelly Custis and George Washington Custis, made necessary the employment of a tutor. One applicant was Noah Webster, who visited Mount Vernon in 1785, but for some reason did not engage. A certain William Shaw had charge for almost a year and then in 1786 Tobias Lear, a native of New Hampshire and a graduate of Harvard, was employed. It is supposed that some of the lessons were taught in the small circular building in the garden; Washington himself refers to it as "the house in the Upper Garden called the School house."

Lear's duties were by no means all pedagogical and ultimately he became Washington's private secretary. In Philadelphia he and his family lived in the presidential mansion. Washington had for him "a particular friendship," an almost fatherly affection. His interest in Lear's little son Lincoln was almost as great as he would have bestowed upon his own grandson. Apropos of the recovery of the child from a serious illness he wrote in 1793: "It gave Mrs. Washington, myself, and all who knew him sincere pleasure to hear that our little favourite had arrived safe and was in good health at Portsmouth—we sincerely wish him a long continuance of the latter—that he may be always as charming and promising as he now is—that he may live to be a comfort and blessing to you—and an ornament to his Country. As a token of my affection for him I send him a ticket in the lottery that's now drawing in the Federal City; if it should be his fortune to draw the Hotel, it will add to the pleasure I feel in giving it."

Truly a rather singular gift for a child, we would think in these days. Let us see how it turned out. The next May Washington wrote to Lear, then in Europe on business for the Potomac Navigation Company, of which he had become president: "Often, through the medium of Mr. Langdon, we hear of your son Lincoln, and with pleasure, that he continues to be the healthy and sprightly child he formerly was. He declared if his ticket should turn up a prize, he would go and live in the Federal City. He did not consider, poor little fellow, that some of the prizes would hardly build him a baby house nor foresee that one of these small tickets would be his lot, having drawn no more than ten dollars."

Lear's first wife had died the year before of yellow fever at the President's house in Philadelphia, and for his second he took the widow of George A. Washington—Fanny—who was a niece of Martha Washington, being a daughter of Anna Dandridge Bassett and Colonel Burwell Bassett. This alliance tended to strengthen the friendly relations between Lear and the General. In Washington's last moments Lear held his dying hand and later penned a noble description of the final scene that reveals a man of high and tender sentiments with a true appreciation of his benefactor's greatness. Washington willed him the use of three hundred sixty acres east of Hunting Creek during life. When Fanny Lear died, Lear married Frances Dandridge Henley, another niece of Mrs. Washington. Lear's descendants still own a quilt made by Martha Washington and given to this niece.

During part at least of Washington's absence in the French war his younger brother John Augustine, described in the General's will as "the intimate friend of my ripened age," had charge of his business affairs and resided at Mount Vernon. The relations with this brother were unusually close and Washington took great interest in John's eldest son Bushrod, who studied law and became an associate justice of the Federal Supreme Court. To Bushrod the General gave his papers, library, the Mansion House Farm and other land and a residuary share in the estate.

I am inclined to believe that during 1757-58 John Augustine did not have charge, as Mount Vernon seems to have been under the oversight of a certain Humphrey Knight, who worked the farm on shares. He was evidently a good farmer, for in 1758 William Fairfax, who kept a friendly eye upon his absent neighbor's affairs, wrote: "You have some of the finest Tobacco & Corn I have seen this year," The summer was, however, exceedingly dry and the crop was good in a relative sense only. Knight tried to keep affairs in good running order and the men hard at work, reporting "as to ye Carpentrs I have minded em all I posably could, and has whipt em when I could see a fault." Knight died September 9, 1758, a few months before Washington's marriage.

Washington's general manager during the Revolution was Lund Washington, a distant relative. He was a man of energy and ability and retired against protests in 1785. Unfortunately not much of the correspondence between the two has come down to us, as Lund destroyed most of the General's letters. Why he did so I do not know, though possibly it was because in them

Washington commented freely about persons and sections. In one that remains, for example, written soon after his assumption of command at Cambridge, the General speaks disparagingly of some New England officers and says of the troops that they may fight well, but are "dirty fellows." When the British visited Mount Vernon in 1781 Lund conciliated them by furnishing them provisions, thereby drawing down upon himself a rebuke from the owner, who said that he would rather have had his buildings burned down than to have purchased their safety in such a way. Nevertheless the General appreciated Lund's services and the two always remained on friendly terms.

Lund was succeeded by Major George Augustine Washington, son of the General's brother Charles. From his youth George Augustine had attached himself to his uncle's service and fought under him in the Revolution, a part of the time on the staff of Lafayette. The General had a strong affection for him and in 1784 furnished him with money to take a trip to the West Indies for his health. Contrary to expectations, he improved, married Fanny Bassett, and for several years resided at Mount Vernon. But the disease, consumption, returned and, greatly to his uncle's distress, he died in 1792. Washington helped to care for the widow until she became the wife of Tobias Lear.

Two other nephews, Robert Lewis and Howell Lewis, were in turn for short intervals in charge of affairs, but presently the estate was committed to the care of an Englishman named Anthony Whiting, who was already overseer of two of the farms. Like his predecessor he was a victim of consumption and died in June, 1793. Washington showed him great kindness, repeatedly urging him not to overexert, to make use of wines, tea, coffee and other delicacies that had been sent for the use of guests. As Whiting was also troubled with rheumatism, the President dropped affairs of state long enough to write him that "Flannel next the skin [is] the best cure for, & preventative of the Rheumatism I have ever tried." Yet after Whiting's death the employer learned that he had been deceived in the man—that he "drank freely—kept bad company at my house in Alexandria—and was a very debauched person."

William Pearce, who followed Whiting, came from the eastern shore of Maryland, where he owned an estate called "Hopewell." His salary was a hundred guineas a year. A poor speller and grammarian, he was nevertheless practical and one of the best of all the managers. He resigned in 1797 on account of rheumatism, which he thought would prevent him from giving business the attention it deserved. Washington parted from him with much regret and gave him a "certificate" in which he spoke in the most laudatory terms of his "honesty, sobriety industry and skill" and stated that his conduct had given "entire satisfaction." They later corresponded occasionally and exchanged farm and family news in the most friendly way.

The last manager, James Anderson, was described by his employer as "an honest, industrious and judicious Scotchman." His salary was one hundred forty pounds a year. Though born in a country where slaves were unknown, he proved adaptable to Virginia conditions and assisted the overseers "in some chastisements when needful." As his employer retired from the presidency soon after he took charge he had not the responsibility of some who had preceded him, for Washington was unwilling to be reduced to a mere cipher on his own estate. Seeing the great profusion of cheap corn and rye, Anderson, who was a good judge of whisky, engaged the General in a distillery, which stood near the grist mill. The returns for 1798 were £344.12.7-3/4, with 755-1/4 gallons still unsold.

Washington's letters to his managers are filled with exhortations and sapient advice about all manner of things. He constantly urged them to avoid familiarities with the blacks and preached the importance of "example," for, "be it good or bad," it "will be followed by all those who look up to you.— Keep every one in their place, & to their duty; relaxation from, or neglect in small matters, lead to like attempts in matters of greater magnitude."

The absent owner was constantly complaining that his managers failed to inform him about matters concerning which he had inquired. Hardly a report reached him that did not fail to explain something in which he was interested. This was one of the many disadvantages of farming at long range.

In 1793 Washington described his overseers to Pearce, who was just taking charge, in great detail. Stuart is competent, sober and industrious, but talkative and conceited. "If he stirs early and works late ... his talkativeness and vanity may be humored." Crow is active and possessed of good judgment, but overly fond of "visiting and receiving visits." McKoy is a "sickly, slothful and stupid fellow." Butler, the gardener, may mean well, but "he has no more authority over the Negroes he is placed over than an old woman would have." Ultimately he dismissed Butler on this ground, but as the man could find no other job he was forced to give him assistance. The owner's opinions of Davy, the colored overseer at Muddy Hole Farm, and of Thomas Green, the carpenter, are given elsewhere.

In the same letter he exhorted Pearce to see what time the overseers "turn out of a morning—for I have strong suspicions that this, with some of them, is at a late hour, the consequences of which to the Negroes is not difficult to foretell. All these Overseers as you will perceive by their agreements, which I here with send, are on standing wages; and this with men who are not actuated by the principles of honor or honesty, and not very regardful of their characters, leads naturally to endulgences—as *their* profits whatever may be *mine*, are the same whether they are at a horse race or on the farm."

From the above it will appear that he did not believe that the overseers were storing up any large treasury of good works. In the Revolution he wrote that one overseer and a confederate, "I believe, divide the profits of my Estate on the York River, tolerably between them, for the devil of anything do I get." Later he approved the course of George A. Washington in depriving an overseer of the privilege of killing four shoats, as this gave him an excuse when caught killing a pig to say that it was one of those to which he was entitled. Even when honest, the overseers were likely to be careless. They often knew little about the stock under their charge and in making their weekly reports would take the number from old reports instead of actually making the count, with the result that many animals could die or disappear long before those in charge became aware of it.

Washington's carpenters were mostly slaves, but

Part of Manger's Weekly Report.

he usually hired a white man to oversee and direct them. In 1768, for example, he engaged for this purpose a certain Jonathan Palmer, who was to receive forty pounds a year, four hundred pounds of meat, twenty bushels of corn, a house to live in, a garden, and also the right to keep two cows.

The carpenters were required not only to build houses, barns, sheds and other structures, but also boats, and had to hew out or whipsaw many of the timbers and boards used.

The carpenter whose name we meet oftenest was Thomas Green, who married Sally Bishop. I have seen a contract signed by Green in 1786, by which he was to receive annually forty-five pounds in Virginia currency, five hundredweight of pork, pasture for a cow, and two hundred pounds of common flour. He also had the right to be absent from the plantation half a day in every month. He did not use these vacations to good advantage, for he was a drunken incompetent and tried Washington's patience sorely. Washington frequently threatened to dismiss him and as often relented and Green finally, in 1794, quit of his own accord, though Washington thereafter had to assist his family.

The employment of white day labor at Mount Vernon was not extensive. In harvest time some extra cradlers were employed, as this was a kind of work at which the slaves were not very skilful. Payment was at the rate of about a dollar a day or a dollar for cutting four acres, which was the amount a skilled man could lay down in a day. The men were also given three meals a day and a pint of spirits each. They slept in the barns, with straw and a blanket for a bed. With them worked the overseers, cutting, binding and setting up the sheaves in stools or shocks.

Laziness in his employees gave our Farmer a vast deal of unhappiness. It was an enemy that he fought longer and more persistently than he fought the British. In his early career a certain "Young Stephens," son of the miller, seems to have been his greatest trial. "Visited my Plantations," he confides to his diary. "Severely reprimanded young Stephens for his Indolence, and his father for suffering it." "Visited my Quarters & ye Mill according to custom found young Stephens absent." "Visited my Plantations and found to my great surprise Stephens constantly at work." "Rid out to my Plantn. and to my Carpenters. Found Richard Stephens hard at work with an ax—very extraordinary this!"

To what extent the change proved permanent we do not know. But even though the reformation was absolute, it mattered little, for each year produces a new crop of lazybones just as it does "lambs" and "suckers."

Enough has been said to show that our Farmer was impatient, perhaps even a bit querulous, but innumerable incidents prove that he was also generous and just. Thus when paper currency depreciated to a low figure he, of his own volition, wrote to Lund Washington that he would not hold him to his contract, but would pay his wages by a share in the crops, and this at a time when his own debtors were discharging their indebtedness in the almost worthless paper.

If ever a square man lived, Washington was that man. He believed in the Golden Rule and he practiced it—not only in church, but in business. It was not for nothing that as a boy he had written as his one hundred tenth "Rule of Civility": "Labor to keep alive in your Breast that Little Spark of Celestial fire called Conscience."

In looking through his later letters I came upon one, dated January 7, 1796, from Pearce stating that Davenport, a miller whom Washington had brought from Pennsylvania, was dead. He had already received six hundred pounds of pork and more wages than were due him as advances for the coming year. What should be done? asked the manager. "His Wife and Children will be in a most Distressed Situation." As I examined the papers that followed I said to myself: "I will see if I know what his answer will be." I thought I did, and so it proved. Back from Philadelphia came the answer:

"Altho' she can have no *right* to the Meat, I would have none of it taken from her.—You may also let her have middlings from the Mill,—and until the house may become indispensably necessary for the succeeding Miller, let her remain in it.—As she went from these parts she can have no friends (by these I mean relations) where she is. If therefore she wishes to return back to his, or her own relations, aid her in doing so."

Not always were his problems so somber as this. Consider, for example, the case of William M. Roberts, an employee who feared that he was about to get the sack. "In your absence to Richmond," writes anxious William, November 25, 1784, "My Wife & I have had a Most Unhappy falling out Which I Shall not Trouble you with the Praticlers No farther than This. I hapened To Git to Drinking one Night as She thought Two Much. & From one Cros Question to a nother Matters weare Carred to the Length it has been. Which Mr. Lund Washington will Inform you For My part I am Heartily Sorry in my Sole My Wife appares to be the Same & I am of a pinion that We Shall Live More Happy than We have Don for the fewter."

In his dealings with servants Washington was sometimes troubled with questions that worry us when we are trying to hire "Mary" or "Bridget." Thus when Mrs. Washington's ill health necessitated his engaging in 1797 a housekeeper he made the following minute and anxious inquiries of Bushrod Washington at Richmond concerning a certain Mrs. Forbes:

"What countrywoman is she?

"Whether Widow or Wife? if the latter

"Where her husband is?

"What family she has?

"What age she is?

"Of what temper?

"Whether active and spirited in the execution of her business?

"Whether sober and honest?

"Whether much knowledge in Cookery, and understands ordering and setting out a Table?

"What her appearance is?

"With other matters which may occur to you to ask,—and necessary for me to know.

"Mrs. Forbes will have a warm, decent and comfortable room to herself, to lodge in, and will eat of the victuals of our Table, but not set at it, at any time *with us*, be her appearance what it may, for if this was *once admitted*, no line satisfactory to either party, perhaps, could be drawn thereafter.—It might be well for me to know however whether this was admitted at Govr. Brookes or not."

Considerate and just though he was, his deliberate judgment of servants after a long and varied experience was that they are "necessary plagues ... they baffle all calculation in the accomplishment of any plan or repairs they are engaged in; and require more attention to and looking after than can be well conceived."

Perhaps the soundest philosophy upon this trying and much debated servant question is that of Miles Standish, who proceeded, however, straightway to violate it.

CHAPTER XII

BLACK SLAVES

It is one of the strange inconsistencies of history that one of the foremost champions of liberty of all time should himself have been the absolute owner and master of men, women and children.

Visitors at Mount Vernon saw many faces there, but only a few were white faces, the rest were those of black slaves. On each farm stood a village of wooden huts, where turbaned mammies crooned and piccaninnies gamboled in the sunshine. The cooks, the house servants, the coachmen, the stable boys, almost all the manual workers were slaves. Even the Mansion House grounds, if the master was away, were apt to be overrun with black children, for though only the progeny of a few house servants were supposed to enter the precincts, the others often disregarded the prohibition, to the destruction of the Farmer's flowers and rare shrubs.

From his father Washington inherited ten or a dozen slaves and, as occasion required or opportunity offered, he added to the number. By 1760 he paid taxes on forty-nine slaves, in 1770 on eighty-seven and in 1774 on one hundred thirty-five. Presently he found himself overstocked and in 1778 expressed a wish to barter for land some "Negroes, of whom I every day long more to get clear of[7]." Still later he declared that he had more negroes than could be employed to advantage on his estate, but was principled against selling any, while hiring them out was almost as bad. "What then is to be done? Something or I shall be ruined."

[7] In 1754 he bought a "fellow" for £40.5, another named Jack for £52.5 and a woman called Clio for £50. Two years later he acquired two negro men and a woman for £86, and from Governor Dinwiddie a woman and child for £60. In 1758 he got Gregory for £60.9. Mount Vernon brought him eighteen more. Mrs. Washington was the owner of a great many slaves, which he called the "dower Negroes," and with part of the money she brought him he acquired yet others. The year of his marriage he bought Will for £50, another fellow for £60, Hannah and child for £80 and nine others for £406. In 1762 he acquired two of Fielding Lewis for £115, seven of Lee Massey for £300, also one-handed Charles for £30. Two years later he bought two men and a woman of the estate of Francis Hobbs for £128.10, the woman being evidently of inferior quality, for she cost only £20. Another slave purchased that year from Sarah Alexander was more valuable, costing £76. Judy and child, obtained of Garvin Corbin, cost £63. Two mulattoes, Will and Frank, bought of Mary Lee in 1768, cost £61.15 and £50, and Will became

famous as a body servant; Adam and Frank, bought of the same owner, cost £38. He bought five more slaves in 1772. Some writers say that this was his last purchase, but it is certain that thereafter he at least took a few in payment of debts.

In 1786 he took a census of his slaves on the Mount Vernon estate. On the Mansion House Farm he had sixty-seven, including Will or Billy Lee, who was his "val de Chambre," two waiters, two cooks, three drivers and stablers, three seamstresses, two house maids, two washers, four spinners, besides smiths, a waggoner, carter, stock keeper, knitters and carpenters. Two women were "almost past service," one of them being "old and almost blind." A man, Schomberg, was "past labour." Lame Peter had been taught to knit. Twenty-six were children, the youngest being Delia and Sally. At the mill were Miller Ben and three coopers. On the whole estate there were two hundred sixteen slaves, including many dower negroes.

If our Farmer took any special pains to develop the mental and moral nature of "My People," as he usually called his slaves, I have found no record of it. Nor is there any evidence that their sexual relations were other than promiscuous—if they so desired. Marriage had no legal basis among slaves and children took the status of their mother. Instances occurred in which couples remained together and had an affection for their families, but the reverse was not uncommon. This state of affairs goes far toward explaining moral lapses among the negroes of to-day.

I have found only one or two lists of the increase of the slaves, one being that transmitted by James Anderson, manager, in February, 1797, to the effect that "there are 3 Negro Children Born, & one dead—at River Farm 1; born at Mansion house, Lina 1; at Union Farm 1 born & one dead—It was killed by Worms. Medical assistance was called—But the mothers are very inattentive to their Young."

Just why the managers, when they carefully mentioned the arrival of calves, colts, lambs and mules, did not also transmit news of the advent of the more valuable two-legged live stock, is not apparent. In many reports, however, in accounting for the time of slaves, occur such entries as: "By Cornelia in child bed 6 days." Occasionally the fact and sex of the increase is mentioned, but not often.

Washington was much more likely to take notice of deaths than of increases. "Dorcas, daughter of Phillis, died, which makes 4 Negroes lost this winter," he wrote in 1760. He strove to safeguard the health of his slaves and employed a physician by the year to attend to them, the payment, during part of the time at least, being fifteen pounds per annum. In 1760 this physician was a certain James Laurie, evidently not a man of exemplary character, for

Washington wrote, April 9, 1760, "Doctr. Laurie came here. I may add Drunk." Another physician was a Doctor Brown, another Doctor William Rumney, and in later years it was Washington's old friend Doctor Craik. I have noticed two instances of Washington's sending slaves considerable distances for medical treatment. One boy, Christopher, bitten by a dog, went to a "specialist" at Lebanon, Pennsylvania, for treatment to avert madness, and another, Tom, had an operation performed on his eyes, probably for cataract.

When at home the Farmer personally helped to care for sick slaves. He had a special building erected near the Mansion House for use as a hospital. Once he went to Winchester in the Shenandoah region especially to look after slaves ill with smallpox "and found everything in the utmost confusion, disorder, and backwardness. Got Blankets and every other requisite from Winchester, and settied things on the best footing I could." As he had had smallpox when at Barbadoes, he had no fear of contagion.

Among the entries in his diary are: "Visited my Plantations and found two negroes sick ... ordered them to be blooded." "Found that lightening had struck my quarters and near 10 Negroes in it, some very bad but by letting blood recovered." "Found the new negro Cupid ill of a pleurisy at Dogue Run Quarter and had him brot home in a cart for better care of him.... Cupid extremely ill all this day and night. When I went to bed I thought him within a few hours of breathing his last." However, Cupid recovered.

In his contracts with overseers Washington stipulated proper care of the slaves. Once he complained to his manager that the generality of the overseers seem to "view the poor creatures in scarcely any other light than they do a draught horse or ox; neglecting them as much when they are unable to work; instead of comforting and nursing them when they lye on a sick bed." Again he wrote:

"When I recommended care of and attention to my negros in sickness, it was that the first stage of, and the whole progress through the disorders with which they might be seized (if more than a slight indisposition) should be closely watched, and timely applications and remedies be administered; especially in the pleurisies, and all inflammatory disorders accompanied with pain, when a few day's neglect, or want of bleeding might render the ailment incurable. In such cases sweeten'd teas, broths and (according to the nature of the complaint, and the doctor's prescription) sometimes a little wine, may be necessary to nourish and restore the patient; and these I am perfectly willing to allow, when it is requisite."

Yet again he complains that the overseers "seem to consider a Negro much in the same light as they do the brute beasts, on the farms, and often times treat them as inhumanly."

His slaves by no means led lives of luxury and inglorious ease. A friendly Polish poet who visited Mount Vernon in 1798 was shocked by the poor quarters and rough food provided for them. He wrote:

"We entered some negroes' huts—for their habitations cannot be called houses. They are far more miserable than the poorest of the cottages of our peasants. The husband and his wife sleep on a miserable bed, the children on the floor. A very poor chimney, a little kitchen furniture amid this misery—a tea-kettle and cups.... A small orchard with vegetables was situated close to the hut. Five or six hens, each with ten or fifteen chickens, walked there. That is the only pleasure allowed to the negroes: they are not permitted to keep either ducks or geese or pigs."

Yet all the slaves he saw seemed gay and light-hearted and on Sundays played at pitching the bar with an activity and zest that indicated that they managed to keep from being overworked and found some enjoyment in life.

To our Farmer's orderly and energetic soul his shiftless lazy blacks were a constant trial. In his diary for February, 1760, he records that four of his carpenters had only hewed about one hundred twenty feet of timber in a day, so he tried the experiment of sitting down and watching them. They at once fell to with such energy and worked so rapidly that he concluded that each one ought to hew about one hundred twenty-five feet per day and more when the days were longer.

A later set of carpenters seem to have been equally trifling, for of them he said in 1795: "There is not to be found so idle a set of Rascals.—In short, it appears to me, that to make even a chicken coop, would employ all of them a week."

"It is observed by the Weekly Report," he wrote when President, "that the Sowers make only Six Shirts a Week, and the last week Caroline (without being sick) made only five;—Mrs. Washington says their usual task was to make nine with Shoulder straps, & good sewing:—tell them therefore from me, that what *has* been done *shall* be done by fair or foul means; & they had better make a choice of the first, for their own reputation, & for the sake of peace and quietness otherwise they will be sent to the several Plantations, & be placed at common labor under the Overseers thereat. Their work ought to be well examined, or it will be most shamefully executed, whether little or much of it is done—and it is said, the same attention ought to be given to Peter (& I suppose to Sarah likewise) or the Stockings will be knit too small for those for whom they are intended; such being the idleness, & deceit of those people."

"What kind of sickness is Betty Davis's?" he demands on another occasion. "If pretended ailments, without apparent causes, or visible effects, will screen her from work, I shall get no work at all from her;—for a more lazy, deceitful and impudent huzzy is not to be found in the United States than she is."

"I observe what you say of Betty Davis &ct," he wrote a little later, "but I never found so much difficulty as you seem to apprehend in distinguishing between *real* and *feigned* sickness;—or when a person is much *afflicted* with pain.—Nobody can be very sick without having a fever, nor will a fever or any other disorder continue long upon any one without reducing them.—Pain also, if it be such as to yield entirely to its force, week after week, will appear by its effects; but my people (many of them) will lay up a month, at the end of which no visible change in their countenance, nor the loss of an oz of flesh, is discoverable; and their allowance of provision is going on as if nothing ailed them."

He not only deemed his negroes lazy, but he had also a low opinion of their honesty. Alexandria was full of low shopkeepers who would buy stolen goods from either blacks or whites, and Washington declared that not more than two or three of his slaves

Spinning House—Last Building to the Right.

would refrain from filching anything upon which they could lay their hands.

He found that he dared not leave his wine unlocked, because the servants would steal two glasses to every one consumed by visitors and then allege that the visitors had drunk it all.

He even suspected the slaves of taking a toll from the clover and timothy seed given them to sow and adopted the practice of having the seed mixed with sand, as that rendered it unsalable and also had the advantage of getting the seed sown more evenly.

Corn houses and meat houses had to be kept locked, apples picked early, and sheep and pigs watched carefully or the slaves took full advantage of the opportunity. Nor can we at this distant day blame them very much or wax so indignant as did their master over their thieveries. They were held to involuntary servitude and if now and then they got the better of their owner and managed to enjoy a few stolen luxuries they merely did a little toward evening the score. But it was poor training for future freedom.

The black picture which Washington draws of slavery—from the master's standpoint—is exceedingly interesting and significant. The character he gives the slaves is commended to the attention of those persons who continually bemoan the fact that freedom and education have ruined the negroes.

One of the famous "Rules of Civility," which the boy Washington so carefully copied, set forth that persons of high degree ought to treat their inferiors "with affibility & Courtesie, without Arrogancy." There is abundant evidence that when he came to manhood he was reasonably considerate of his slaves, and yet he was a Master and ruled them in martinet fashion. His advice to a manager was to keep the blacks at a proper distance, "for they will grow upon familiarity in proportion as you will sink in authority." The English farmer Parkinson records that the first time he walked with General Washington among his negroes he was amazed at the rough manner in which he spoke to them. This does not mean that Washington cursed his negroes as the mate of a Mississippi River boat does his roustabouts, but I suspect that those who have heard such a mate can form an idea of the *tone* employed by our Farmer that so shocked Parkinson. Military officers still employ it toward their men.

Corporal punishment was resorted to on occasion, but not to extremes. The Master writes regarding a runaway: "Let Abram get his deserts when taken, by way of example; but do not trust to Crow to give it to him;—for I have reason to believe he is swayed more by passion than by judgment in all his corrections." Tradition says that on one occasion he found an overseer brutally beating one of the blacks and, indignant at the sight, sprang from his horse and, whip in hand, strode up to the overseer, who was so affrighted that he backed away crying loudly: "Remember your character, General, remember your character!" The General paused, reprimanded the overseer for cruelty and rode off.

Among his slaves were some that were too unruly to be managed by ordinary means. In the early seventies he had such a one on a plantation in York County, Will Shag by name, who was a persistent runaway, and who whipped the overseer and was obstreperous generally. Another slave committed so serious an offense that he was tried under state law and >>vas executed. When a bondman became particularly fractious he was threatened with being sent to the West Indies, a place held in as much dread as was "down the river" in later years. In 1766 Washington sent such a fellow off and to the captain of the ship that carried the slave away he wrote:

"With this letter comes a negro (Tom) which I beg the favor of you to sell in any of the islands you may go to, for whatever he will fetch, and bring me in return for him

"One hhd of best molasses

"One ditto of best rum

"One barrel of lymes, if good and cheap

"One pot of tamarinds, containing about 10 lbs.

"Two small ditto of mixed sweetmeats, about 5 lbs. each. And the residue, much or little, in good old spirits. That this fellow is both a rogue and a runaway (tho he was by no means remarkable for the former, and never practiced the latter till of late) I shall not pretend to deny. But that he is exceedingly healthy, strong, and good at the hoe, the whole neighborhood can testify, and particularly Mr. Johnson and his son, who have both had him under them as foreman of the gang; which gives me reason to hope that he may with your good management sell well, if kept clean and trim'd up a little when offered for sale."

Another "misbehaving fellow" named Waggoner Jack was sent off in 1791 and was sold for "one pipe and Quarter Cask" of wine. Somewhat later (1793) Matilda's Ben became addicted to evil courses and among other things committed an assault and battery on Sambo, for which he received corporal punishment duly approved by our Farmer, whose earnest desire it was "that quarrels be stopped." Evidently the remedy was insufficient, for not long after the absent owner wrote:

"I am very sorry that so likely a fellow as Matilda's Ben should addict himself to such courses as he is pursuing. If he should be guilty of any atrocious crime that would affect his life, he might be given up to the civil authority for trial; but for such offenses as most of his color are guilty of, you had better try further correction, accompanied by admonition and advice. The two latter sometimes succeed where the first has failed. He, his father and mother (who I dare say are his receivers) may be told in explicit language, that if a stop is not put to his rogueries and other villainies, by fair means and shortly, that I will ship him off (as I did Waggoner Jack) for the West Indies, where he will have no opportunity of playing such pranks as he is at present engaged in."

A few of the negroes occupied positions of some trust and responsibility. One named Davy was for many years manager of Muddy Hole Farm, and Washington thought that he carried on his work as well as did the white overseers and more quietly than some, though rather negligent of live stock. Each year at killing time he was allowed two or three hundredweight of pork as well as other privileges not accorded to the ordinary slave. Still his master did not entirely trust him, for in 1795 we find that Washington suspected Davy of having stolen some lambs that had been reported as "lost."

The most famous of the Mount Vernon negroes was William Lee, better known as Billy, whose purchase from Mary Lee has already been noticed. Billy was Washington's valet and huntsman and served with him throughout the Revolution as a body servant, rode with him at reviews and was painted by Savage in the well-known group of the President and his family. Naturally Billy put on airs and presumed a good deal upon his position. On one occasion at Monmouth the General and his staff were reconnoitering the British, and Billy and fellow valets gathered on an adjoining hill beneath a sycamore tree whence Billy, telescope in hand, surveyed the enemy with much importance and interest. Washington, with a smile, called the attention of his aides to the spectacle. About the same time the British, noticing the group of horsemen and unable to distinguish the color of the riders, paid their respects to Billy and his followers in the shape of a solid shot, which went crashing through the top of the tree, whereupon there was a rapid recession of coat tails toward the rear.

Billy was a good and faithful servant and his master appreciated the fact. In 1784 we find Washington writing to his Philadelphia agent: "The mullatto fellow, William, who has been with me all the war, is attached (married he says) to one of his own color, a free woman, who during the war, was also of my family. She has been in an infirm condition for some time, and I had conceived that the connexion between them had ceased; but I am mistaken it seems; they are both applying to get her here, and tho' I never wished to see her more, I can not refuse his request (if it can be complied with on reasonable terms) as he has served me faithfully for many years. After premising this much, I have to beg the favor of you to procure her a passage to Alexandria."

Next year while Billy and his master were engaged in surveying a piece of ground he fell and broke his knee pan, with the result that he was crippled ever after. When Washington started to New York in 1789 to be inaugurated Billy insisted upon accompanying him, but gave out on the way and was left at Philadelphia. A little later, by the President's direction, Lear wrote to return Billy to Mount Vernon, "for he cannot be of any service here, and perhaps will require a person to attend upon him constantly ... but if he is still anxious to come on here the President would gratify him, altho' he will be troublesome—He has been an old and faithful Servant, this is enough for the President to gratify him in every reasonable wish."

When Billy was at Mount Vernon he worked as a shoemaker. He kept careful note of visitors to the place and if one arrived who had served in the Revolution he invariably received a summons to visit the old negro and as invariably complied. Then would ensue a talk of war experiences which both would enjoy, for between those who had experienced the cold at Valley Forge and the warmth of Monmouth there were ties that reached beyond the narrow confines of caste and color. And upon departure the visitor would leave a coin in Billy's not unwilling palm.

As later noted in detail, Washington made special provision for Billy in his will, and for years the old negro lived upon his annuity. He was much addicted to drink and now and then, alas, had attacks in which he saw things that were not. On such occasions it was customary to send for another mulatto named Westford, who would relieve him by letting a little blood. There came a day when Westford arrived and proceeded to perform his customary office, but the blood refused to flow. Billy was dead.

Washington's kindness to Billy was more or less paralleled by his treatment of other servants. Even when President he would write letters for his slaves to their wives and "Tel Bosos" and would inclose them with his own letters to Mount Vernon. He appreciated the fact that slaves were capable of human feelings like other men and in 1787, when trying to purchase a mason, he instructed his agent not to buy if by so doing he would "hurt the man's feelings" by breaking family ties. Even when dying, noting black Cristopher by his bed, he directed him to sit down and rest. It was a little thing, but kindness is largely made up of little things.

The course taken by him in training a personal servant is indicated by some passages from his correspondence. Writing from the Capital to Pearce, December, 1795, regarding a young negro, Washington says:

"If Cyrus continues to give evidence of such qualities as would fit him for a waiting man, encourage him to persevere in them; and if they should appear to be sincere and permanent, I will receive him in that character when I retire from public life if not sooner.—To be sober, attentive to his duty, honest, obliging and cleanly, are the qualifications necessary to fit him for my purposes.—If he possess these, or can acquire them—he might become useful to me, at the same time that he would exalt, and benefit himself."

"I would have you again stir up the pride of Cyrus," he wrote the next May, "that he may be the fitter for my purposes against I come home; sometime before which (that is as soon as I shall be able to fix on time) I will direct him to be taken into the house, and clothes to be made for him.—In the meanwhile, get him a strong horn comb and direct him to keep his head well combed, that the hair, or wool may grow long."

Once when President word reached his ears that he was being criticized for not furnishing his slaves with sufficient food. He hurriedly directed that the amount should be increased and added: "I will not have my feelings hurt with complaints of this sort, nor lye under the imputation of starving my negros, and thereby driving them to the necessity of thieving to supply the deficiency. To prevent waste or embezzlement is the only inducement to allowancing them at all—for if, instead of a peck they could eat a bushel of meal a week fairly, and required it, I would not withold or begrudge it them."

There is good reason to believe that Washington was respected and even beloved by many of his "People." Colonel Humphreys, who was long at Mount Vernon arranging the General's papers, wrote descriptive of the return at the close of the Revolution:

> "When that foul stain of manhood, slavery, flowed,
> Through Afric's sons transmitted in the blood;
> Hereditary slaves his kindness shar'd,
> For manumission by degrees prepared:
> Return'd from war, I saw them round him press
> And all their speechless glee by artless signs express."

On the whole we must conclude that the lot of the Mount Vernon slaves was a reasonably happy one. The regulations to which they had to conform were rigorous. Their Master strove to keep them at work and to prevent them from "night walking," that is running about at night visiting. Their work was rough, and even the women were expected to labor in the fields plowing, grubbing and hauling manure as if they were men. But they had rations of corn meal, salt pork and salt fish, whisky and rum at Christmas, chickens and vegetables raised by themselves and now and then a toothsome pig sequestered from the Master's herd. When the annual races were held at Alexandria they were permitted to go out into the world and gaze and gabble to their heart's content. And, not least of all, an inscrutable Providence had vouchsafed to Ham one great compensation that whatever his fortune or station he should usually be cheerful. The negro has not that "sad lucidity of mind" that curses his white cousin and leads to general mental wretchedness and suicide.

Some of the Mount Vernon slaves were of course more favored than were others. The domestic and personal servants lived lives of culture and inglorious ease compared with those of the field hands. They formed the aristocracy of colored Mount Vernon society and gave themselves airs accordingly.

Nominally our Farmer's slaves were probably all Christians, though I have found no mention in his papers of their spiritual state. But tradition says that some of them at Dogue Run at least were Voudoo or "conjuring" negroes.

Washington owned slaves and lived his life under the institution of slavery, but he loved it not. He was too honest and keen-minded not to realize that the institution did not square with the principles of human liberty for which he had fought, and yet the problem of slavery was so vast and complicated that he was puzzled how to deal with it. But as early as 1786 he wrote to John F. Mercer, of Virginia: "I never mean, unless some particular circumstances should compel me to it, to possess another slave by purchase, it being among my *first* wishes to see some plan adopted by which slavery in this country may be abolished by law." The running away of his colored cook a decade later subjected him to such trials that he wrote that he would probably have to break his resolution. He did, in fact, carry on considerable correspondence to that end and seems to have taken one man on trial, but I have found no evidence that he discovered a negro that suited him.

In 1794, in explaining to Tobias Lear his reasons for desiring to sell some of his western lands, he said: "*Besides these I have another motive which* makes me earnestly wish for these things—it is indeed more powerful than all the rest—namely to liberate a certain species of property which I possess very repugnantly to my own feelings; but which imperious necessity compels, and until I can substitute some other expedient, by which expenses, not in my power to avoid (however well I may be disposed to do it) can be defrayed."

Later in the same year he wrote to General Alexander Spotswood: "With respect to the other species of property, concerning which you ask my opinion, I shall frankly declare to you that I do not like even to think, much less to talk of it.—However, as you have put the question, I shall, in a few words, give *my ideas* about it.—Were it not then, that I am principled agt. selling negroes, as you would cattle at a market, I would not in twelve months from this date, be possessed of one as a slave.—I shall be happily mistaken, if they are not found to be a very troublesome species of property ere many years pass over our heads."

"I wish from my soul that the Legislature of the State could see the policy of a gradual abolition of slavery," he wrote to Lawrence Lewis three years later. "It might prevent much future mischief."

His ideas on the subject were in accord with those of many other great Southerners of his day such as Madison and Jefferson. These men realized the inconsistency of slavery in a republic dedicated to the proposition that all men are created equal, and vaguely they foresaw the irrepressible conflict that was to divide their country and was to be fought out on a hundred bloody battle-fields. They did not attempt to defend slavery as other than a temporary institution to be eliminated whenever means and methods could be found to do it. Not until the cotton gin had made slavery more profitable and radical abolitionism arose in the North did Southerners of prominence begin to champion slavery as praiseworthy and permanent.

And yet, though Washington in later life deplored slavery, he was human and illogical enough to dislike losing his negroes and pursued runaways with energy. In October, 1760, he spent seven shillings in advertising for an absconder, and the next year paid a minister named Green four pounds for taking up a runaway. In 1766 he advertised rewards for the capture of "Negro Tom," evidently the man he later sold in the West Indies. The return of Henry in 1771 cost him £1.16. Several slaves were carried away by the British during the Revolution and seem never to have been recovered, though the treaty of peace provided for the return of such slaves, and Washington made inquiries concerning them. In 1796, apropos of a girl who had absconded to New England, he excused his desire to recapture her on the ground that as long as slavery was in existence it was hardly fair to allow some to escape and to hold others.

A rather peculiar situation arose in 1791 with regard to some of his "People," His attorney general, Randolph, had taken some slaves to Philadelphia, and the blacks took advantage of the fact that under Pennsylvania law they could not be forced to leave the state against their will. Fearing that some of his own servants might do likewise, Washington directed Lear to get the slaves back to Mount Vernon and to accomplish it "under pretext that may deceive both them and the Public," which goes to show that even George Washington had some of the guile of the serpent.

During this period he was loath to bring the fact that he was a slaveholder too prominently before the public, for he realized the prejudice already existing against the institution in the North. When one of his men absconded in 1795 he gave instructions not to let his name appear in any advertisement of the runaway, at least not north of Virginia.

His final judgment on slavery is expressed in his will. "Upon the decease of my wife it is my will and desire," he wrote, "that all the slaves which I hold *in my own right* shall receive their freedom—To emancipate them during her life, would tho earnestly wished by me, be attended with such insuperable difficulties, on account of their intermixture by marriages with the Dower negroes as to excite the most painful sensations,—if not disagreeable consequences from the latter, while both descriptions are in the occupancy of the same proprietor, it not being in my power under the tenure by which the dower Negroes are held to manumit them."

The number of his own slaves at the time of his death was one hundred twenty-four. Of dower negroes there were one hundred fifty-three, and besides he had forty leased from a Mrs. French.

He expressly forbade the sale of any slave or his transportation out of Virginia, and made provision for the care of the aged, the young and the infirm. He gave immediate freedom to his mulatto man, calling himself William Lee, or if he should prefer it, being physically incapacitated, he might remain in slavery. In either case he was to have an annuity of thirty dollars and the "victuals and cloaths he has been accustomed to receive." "This I give him as a testimony of my sense of his attachment to me and for his faithful services during the revolutionary War."

As a matter of fact, Mrs. Washington preferred to free her own and the General's negroes as soon as possible and it was accordingly done before her death, which occurred in 1802.

One of the servants thus freed, by name Cary, lived to the alleged age of one hundred fourteen years and finally died in Washington City. He was a personage of considerable importance among the colored population of the Capital, and on Fourth of July and other parades would always appear in an old military coat, cocked hat and huge cockade presented by his Master. His funeral was largely attended even by white persons.

CHAPTER XIII

THE FARMER'S WIFE

Martha Dandridge's first husband was a man much older than herself and her second was almost a year younger. Before she embarked upon her second matrimonial venture she had been the mother of four children, and having lost two of these, her husband, her father and mother, she had known, though only twenty-seven, most of the vital experiences that life can give. Perhaps it was well, for thereby she was better fitted to be the mate of a man sober and sedate in disposition and created by Nature to bear heavy burdens of responsibility.

In view of the important places her husband filled, it is astonishing how little we really know of her. Washington occasionally refers to her in his letters and diaries, but usually in an impersonal way that gives us little insight into her character or activities. She purposely destroyed almost all the correspondence that passed between her and her husband and very little else remains that she wrote. From the few letters that do survive it is apparent that her education was slender, though no more so than that of most women of her day even in the upper class. She had a fondness for phonetic spelling, and her verbs and subjects often indulged in family wrangles. She seems to have been conscious of her deficiencies in this direction or at least to have disliked writing, for not infrequently the General acted as her amanuensis. But she was well trained in social and domestic accomplishments, could dance and play on the spinet—in short, was brought up a "gentlewoman." That she must in youth have possessed charm of person and manners is indicated by her subjugation of Daniel Parke Custis, a man of the world and of much greater fortune than herself, and by her later conquest of Washington, for, though it be admitted in the latter case that George may not have objected to her fortune, we can not escape the conclusion that he truly loved her.

In fact, the match seems to have been ideally successful in every respect except one. The contracting parties remained reasonably devoted to each other until the end and though tradition says that Martha would sometimes read George a curtain lecture after they had retired from company, there remains no record of any serious disagreement. Though not brilliant nor possessed of a profound mind, she was a woman of much good sense with an understanding heart. Nor did she lack firmness or public spirit. Edmund

Pendleton relates that when on his way to the Continental Congress in 1774 he stopped at Mount Vernon, "She talked like a Spartan mother to her son on going to battle. 'I hope you will all stand firm—I know George will,' she said."

The poorest artisan in Boston with nothing to lose but his life did not embrace the patriot cause with any greater eagerness than did these Washingtons with their broad acres and thousands of pounds on bond.

There is every reason to believe that Martha Washington was helpful to her husband in many ways. At home she was a good housewife and when Washington was in public life she played her part well. No brilliant sallies of wit spoken by her on any occasion have come down to us, but we know that at Valley Forge she worked day and night knitting socks, patching garments and making shirts for the loyal band of winter patriots who stood by their leader and their cause in the darkest hour of the Revolution.

A Norristown lady who paid her a call in the little stone house that still stands beside the Schuylkill relates that "as she was said to be so grand a lady, we thought we must put on our best bibs and bands. So we dressed ourselves in our most elegant ruffles and silks, and were introduced to her ladyship. And don't you think we found her *knitting with a specked apron on!* She received us very graciously, and easily, but after the compliments were over, she resumed her knitting."

But the marriage was a failure in that there were no children. No doubt both wanted them, for Washington was fond of young people and many anecdotes are handed down of his interest in little tots. Some one has remarked that he was deprived of offspring in order that he might become the Father of His Country.

Toward those near and dear to her Martha Washington was almost foolishly affectionate. In one of her letters she tells of a visit "in Westmoreland whare I spent a weak very agreabley. I carred my little patt with me and left Jackey at home for a trial to see how well I coud stay without him though we ware gon but won fortnight I was quite impatiant to get home. If I at aney time heard the doggs barke or a noise out, I thought thair was a person sent for me. I often fancied he was sick or some accident had happened to him so that I think it is impossible for me to leave him as long as Mr. Washington must stay when he comes down."

Any parent who has been absent from home under similar circumstances and who has imagined the infinite variety of dreadful things that might befall a loved child will sympathize with the mother's heart—in spite of the poor spelling!

Patty Custis was an amiable and beautiful girl who when she grew up came to be called "the dark lady." But she was delicate in health. Some writers have said that she had consumption, but as her stepfather repeatedly called it "Fits," I think it is certain that it was some form of epilepsy. Her parents did everything possible to restore her, but in vain. Once they took her to Bath, now Berkeley Springs, for several weeks and the expenses of that journey we find all duly set down by Colonel Washington in the proper place. As Paul Leicester Ford remarks, some of the remedies tried savored of quackery. In the diary, for February 16, 1770, we learn that "Joshua Evans who came here last Night put an iron Ring upon Patey and went away after Breakfast." Perhaps Evans failed to make the ring after the old medieval rule from three nails or screws that had been taken from a disinterred coffin. At any rate the ring did poor Patty little good and a year later "Mr. Jno. Johnson who has a nostrum for Fits came here in the afternoon." In the spring of 1773 the dark lady died.

Her death added considerably to Washington's possessions, but there is every evidence that he gave no thought to that aspect of the matter. "Her delicate health, or perhaps her fond affection for the only father she had ever known, so endeared her to the 'general', that he knelt at her dying bed, and with a passionate burst of tears prayed aloud that her life might be spared, unconscious that even then her spirit had departed." The next day he wrote to his brother-in-law: "It is an easier matter to conceive than describe the distress of this Family: especially that of the unhappy Parent of our Dear Patey Custis, when I inform you that yesterday removed the Sweet Innocent Girl [who] Entered into a more happy & peaceful abode than any she has met with in the afflicted Path she hitherto has trod."

Before this John Parke Custis, or "Jacky," had given his stepfather considerable anxiety. Jacky's mind turned chiefly from study to dogs, horses and guns and, in an effort, to "make him fit for more useful purposes than horse races," Washington put him under the tutorship of an Anglican clergyman named Jonathan Boucher, who endeavored to instruct some of the other gilded Virginia youths of his day. But Latin and Greek were far less interesting to the boy than the pretty eyes of Eleanor Calvert and the two entered into a clandestine engagement. In all respects save one the match was eminently satisfactory, for the Calvert family, being descended from Lord Baltimore, was as good as any in America, and Miss Nelly's amiable qualities, wrote Washington, had endeared her to her prospective relations, but both were very young, Jack being about seventeen, and the girl still younger. While consenting to the match, therefore, Washington insisted that its consummation should be postponed for two years and packed the boy off to King's College, now Columbia. But Martha Washington was a fond and doting mother and, as Patty's death occurred almost immediately, Jack's absence in distant New York was more than she could bear. He was, therefore, allowed to return home in three months instead of two years, and in February, 1774, was wedded to the girl of his choice. Mrs. Washington felt the loss of her daughter too keenly to attend, but sent this message by her husband:

"MY DEAR NELLY.—God took from me a Daughter when June Roses were blooming—He has now given me another Daughter about her Age when Winter winds are blowing, to warm my Heart again. I am as Happy as One so Afflicted and so Blest can be. Pray receive my Benediction and a wish that you may long live the Loving Wife of my happy Son, and a Loving Daughter of

"Your affectionate Mother,

"M. WASHINGTON."

The marriage, it may be added here, sobered John Custis. He and his bride established themselves at Abingdon on the Potomac, not far from Mount Vernon, and with their little ones were often visitors, especially when the General was away to the war and Mrs. Washington was alone. Toward the close of the war Jack himself entered the army, rose to the rank of colonel and died of fever contracted in the siege of Yorktown. Thus again was the mother's heart made sorrowful, nor did the General himself accept the loss unmoved. He at once adopted the two youngest children, Eleanor and George Washington Parke, and brought them up in his own family.

Eleanor Custis, or "Nelly," as she was affectionately called, grew up a joyous, beautiful cultured girl, who won the hearts of all who saw her. The Polish poet, Julian Niemcewicz, who visited Mount Vernon in 1798, wrote of her as "the divine Miss Custis…. She was one of those celestial beings so rarely produced by nature, sometimes dreamt of by poets and painters, which one cannot see without a feeling of ecstasy." As already stated, she married the General's nephew, Lawrence Lewis. In September, 1799, Washington told the pair that they might build a house on Grey's Heights on the Dogue Run Farm and rent the farm, "by all odds the best and most productive I possess," promising that on his death the place should go to them. Death came before the house was built, but later the pair erected on the Heights "Woodlawn," one of the most beautiful and pretentious places in Fairfax County.

George Washington Parke Custis grew up much such a boy as his father was. He took few matters seriously and neglected the educational opportunities thrown in his way. Washington said of him that "from his infancy I have discovered an almost unconquerable disposition to indolence in everything that did not tend to his amusements." But he loved the boy, nevertheless, and late in life Custis confessed, "we have seen him shed tears of parental solicitude over the manifold errors and follies of our unworthy youth." The boy had a good heart, however, and if he was the source of worry to the great man during the great man's life, he at least did what he could to keep the great man's memory green. He wrote a book of recollections full of filial affection and Latin phrases and painted innumerable war pictures in which Washington was always in the foreground on a white horse "with the British streaking it." Washington bequeathed to him a square in the City of Washington and twelve hundred acres on Four Mile Run in the vicinity of Alexandria. Upon land near by inherited from his father Custis built the famous Arlington mansion, almost ruining himself financially in doing so. Upon his death the estate fell to his daughter, Mrs. Robert E. Lee, and it is now our greatest national cemetery.

Mrs. Washington not only managed the Mount Vernon household, but she looked after the spinning of yarn, the weaving of cloth and the making of clothing for the family and for the great horde of slaves. At times, particularly during the Revolution and the non-importation days that preceded it, she had as many as sixteen spinning-wheels in operation at once. The work was done in a special spinning house, which was well equipped with looms, wheels, reels, flaxbrakes and other machinery. Most of the raw material, such as wool and flax and sometimes even cotton, was produced upon the place and never left it until made up into the finished product.

In 1768 the white man and five negro girls employed in the work produced 815-3/4 yards of linen, 365-1/4 yards of woolen cloth, 144 yards of linsey and 40 yards of cotton cloth. With his usual pains Washington made a comparative statement of the cost of this cloth produced at home and what it would have cost him if it had been purchased in England, and came to the conclusion that only £23.19.11 would be left to defray the expense of spinning, hire of the six persons engaged, "cloathing, victualling, wheels, &c." Still the work was kept going.

A great variety of fabrics were produced: "striped woolen, wool plaided, cotton striped, linen, wool-birdseye, cotton filled with wool, linsey, M's and O's, cotton Indian dimity, cotton jump stripe, linen filled with tow, cotton striped with silk, Roman M., janes twilled, huccabac, broadcloth, counterpain, birdseye diaper, Kirsey wool, barragon, fustian, bed-ticking, herringbox, and shalloon."

In non-importation days Mrs. Washington even made the cloth for two of her own gowns, using cotton striped with silk, the latter being obtained from the ravellings of brown silk stockings and crimson damask chair covers.

The housewife believed in good cheer and an abundance of it, and the larders at Mount Vernon were kept well filled. Once the General protested to Lund Washington because so many hogs had been killed, whereupon the manager replied that when he put up the meat he had expected that Mrs. Washington would have been at home and that he knew there would be need for it because her

Weekly Report on the Work of the Spinners.

"charitable disposition is in the same proportion as her meat house."

She had a swarm of relatives by blood and marriage and they visited her long and often. The Burwells, the Bassetts, the Dandridges and all the rest came so frequently that hardly a week passed that at least one of them did not sleep beneath the hospitable roof. Even her stepmother paid her many visits and, what is more, was strongly urged by the General to make the place her permanent home. When Mrs. Washington was at home during the Revolution her son and her daughter-in-law spent most of their time there. After the Revolution her two youngest grandchildren resided at Mount Vernon, and the two older ones, Elizabeth and Martha, were often there, as was their mother, who married as her second husband Doctor Stuart, a man whom Washington highly esteemed.

It would be foolish to deny that Mrs. Washington did not take pleasure in the honors heaped upon her husband or that she did not enjoy the consideration that accrued to her as First Lady of the Land. Yet public life at times palled upon her and she often spoke of the years of the presidency as her "lost days." New York and Philadelphia, she said, were "not home, only a sojourning. The General and I feel like children just released from school or from a hard taskmaster.... How many dear friends I have left behind! They fill my memory with sweet thoughts. Shall I ever see them again? Not likely unless they come to me, for the twilight is gathering around our lives. I am again fairly settled down to the pleasant duties of an old-fashioned Virginia-housekeeper, steady as a clock, busy as a bee, and cheerful as a cricket."

That she did not overdraw her account of her industry is borne out by a Mrs. Carrington, who, with her husband, one of the General's old officers, visited Mount Vernon about this time. She wrote:

"Let us repair to the Old Lady's room, which is precisely in the style of our good old Aunt's—that is to say, nicely fixed for all sorts of work—On one side sits the chambermaid, with her knitting—on the other, a little colored pet learning to sew, an old decent woman, with her table and shears, cutting out the negroes' winter clothes, while the good old lady directs them all, incessantly knitting herself and pointing out to me several pair of nice colored stockings and gloves she had just finished, and presenting me with a pair half done, which she begs I will finish and wear for her. Her netting too is a great source of amusement and is so neatly done that all the family are proud of trimming their dresses with it."

This domestic life was dear to the heart of our Farmer's wife, yet the home-coming did not fail to awaken some melancholy memories. To Mrs. George Fairfax in England she wrote, or rather her husband wrote for her: "The changes which have taken place in this country since you left it (and it is pretty much the case in all other parts of this State) are, in one word, total. In Alexandria, I do not believe there lives at this day a single family with whom you had the smallest acquaintance. In our neighborhood Colo. Mason, Colo. McCarty and wife, Mr. Chickester, Mr. Lund Washington and all the Wageners, have left the stage of human life; and our visitors on the Maryland side are gone and going likewise."

How many people have had like thoughts! One of the many sad things about being the "last leaf upon the tree" is having to watch the other leaves shrivel and drop off and to be left at last in utter loneliness.

Like her husband, Mrs. Washington was an early riser, and it was a habit she seems to have kept up until the end. She rose with the sun and after breakfast invariably retired to her room for an hour of prayer and reading the Scriptures. Her devotions over she proceeded with the ordinary duties of the day.

She seems to have been somewhat fond of ceremony and to have had a considerable sense of personal dignity. A daughter of Augustine Washington, who when twelve years of age spent several weeks at Mount Vernon, related when an old woman that every morning precisely at eleven o'clock the mistress of the mansion expected her company to assemble in the drawing-room, where she greeted them with much formality and kept them an hour on their good behavior. When the clock struck twelve she would rise and ascend to her chamber, returning thence precisely at one, followed by a black servant carrying an immense bowl of punch, from which the guests were expected to partake before dinner. Some of the younger girls became curious to discover why her "Ladyship" retired so invariably to her room, so they slipped out from where she was entertaining their mothers, crept upstairs and hid under her bed. Presently Lady Washington entered and took a seat before a large table. A man-servant then brought a large empty bowl, also lemons, sugar, spices and rum, with which she proceeded to prepare the punch. The young people under the bed thereupon fell to giggling until finally she became aware of their presence. Much offended, or at least pretending to be, she ordered them from the room. They retired with such precipitancy that one of them fell upon the stairway and broke her arm.

Another story is to the effect that one morning Nelly Custis, Miss Dandridge and some other girls who were visiting Nelly came down to breakfast dressed dishabille and with their hair done up in curl papers. Mrs. Washington did not rebuke them and the meal proceeded normally until the announcement was made that some French officers of rank and young Charles Carroll, of Carrollton, who was interested in Miss Custis, had driven up outside, whereupon the foolish virgins sprang up to leave the room in order to make more conventional toilets. But Mrs. Washington forbade their doing so, declaring that what was good enough for General Washington was good enough for any guest of his.

She spoiled George Washington Custis as she had his father, but was more severe with Eleanor or Nelly. Washington bought the girl a fine imported harpsichord, which cost a thousand dollars and which is still to be seen at Mount Vernon, and the grandmother made Nelly practise upon it four or five hours a day. "The poor girl," relates her brother, "would play and cry, and cry and play, for long hours, under the immediate eye of her grandmother." For no shirking was allowed.

The truth would seem to be that Lady Washington was more severe with the young—always excepting Jacky and George—than was her husband. He would often watch their games with evident enjoyment and would encourage them to continue their amusements and not to regard him. He was the confidant of their hopes and fears and even amid tremendous cares of state found time to give advice about their love affairs. For he was a very human man, after all, by no means the marble statue sculptured by some historians.

Yet no doubt Mrs. Washington's severity proceeded from a sense of duty and the fitness of things rather than from any harshness of heart. The little old lady who wrote: "Kiss Marie. I send her two handkerchiefs to wipe her nose," could not have been so very terrible!

She was beloved by her servants and when she left Mount Vernon for New York in 1789 young Robert Lewis reported that "numbers of these poor wretches seemed most affected, my aunt equally so." At Alexandria she stopped at Doctor Stuart's, the home of two of her grandchildren, and next morning there was another affecting scene, such as Lewis never again wished to witness—"the family in tears—the children a-bawling—& everything in the most lamentable situation."

Although she was not the paragon that some writers have pictured, she was a splendid home-loving American woman, brave in heart and helpful to her husband, neither a drone nor a drudge—in the true Scriptural sense a worthy woman who sought wool and flax and worked willingly with her hands. As such her price was far beyond rubies.

As has been remarked before, no brilliant sayings from her lips have been transmitted to posterity. But I suspect that the shivering soldiers on the bleak hillsides at Valley Forge found more comfort in the warm socks she knitted than they could have in the *bon mots* of a Madame de Stael or in the grace of a Josephine and that her homely interest in their welfare tied their hearts closer to their Leader and their Country.

It is not merely because she was the wife of the Hero of the Revolution and the first President of the Republic that she is the most revered of all American women.

CHAPTER XIV

A FARMER'S AMUSEMENTS

No one would ever think of characterizing George Washington as frivolous minded, but from youth to old age he was a believer in the adage that all work and no play makes Jack a dull boy—a saying that many an overworked farmer of our own day would do well to take to heart.

Like most Virginians he was decidedly a social being and loved to be in the company of his kind. This trait was noticeable in his youth and during his early military career, nor did it disappear after he married and settled down at Mount Vernon. Until the end he and Mrs. Washington kept open house, and what a galaxy of company they had! Scarcely a day passed without some guest crossing their hospitable threshold, nor did such visitors come merely to leave their cards or to pay fashionable five-minute calls. They invariably stayed to dinner and most generally for the night; very often for days or weeks at a time. After the Revolution the number of guests increased to such an extent that Mount Vernon became "little better than a well-resorted inn."

Artists came to paint the great man's picture; the sculptor Houdon to take the great man's bust, arriving from Alexandria, by the way, after the family had gone to bed; the Marquis de Lafayette to visit his old friend; Mrs. Macaulay Graham to obtain material for her history; Noah Webster to consider whether he would become the tutor of young Custis; Mr. John Fitch, November 4, 1785, "to propose a draft & Model of a machine for promoting Navigation by means of a Steam"; Charles Thomson, secretary of the Continental Congress, to notify the General of his election to the presidency; a host of others, some out of friendship, others from mere curiosity or a desire for free lodging.

The visit of Lafayette was the last he made to this country while the man with whose fame his name is inseparably linked remained alive. He visited Mount Vernon in August, 1784, and again three months later. When the time for a final adieu came Washington accompanied him to Annapolis and saw him on the road to Baltimore. The generous young benefactor of America was very dear to Washington, and the parting affected him exceedingly. Soon after he wrote to the departed friend a letter in which he showed his heart in a way that was rare with him. "In the moment of our separation," said he, "upon the road as I travelled, and every hour since, I have felt all the love, respect, and attachment for you with which length of years, close connexion, and your merits have inspired me. I have often asked myself, as our carriages separated, whether that was the last sight I ever should have of you."

It was a true foreboding. Often in times that followed Washington was to receive tidings of his friend's triumphs and perilous adventures amid the bloody turmoil of the French Revolution, was to entertain his son at Mount Vernon when the father lay in the dark dungeons of Olmütz, but was never again to look into his face. Years later the younger man, revisiting the grateful Republic he had helped to found, was to turn aside from the acclaiming plaudits of admiring multitudes and stand pensively beside the Tomb of his Leader and reflect upon the years in which they had stood gloriously shoulder to shoulder in defense of a noble cause.

Even when Washington was at the seat of government many persons stopped at Mount Vernon and were entertained by the manager. Several times the absent owner sent wine and other luxuries for the use of such guests. When he was at home friends, relatives, diplomats, delegations of Indians to visit the Great White Father swarmed thither in shoals. In 1797 young Lafayette and his tutor, Monsieur Frestel, whom Washington thought a very sensible man, made the place, by invitation, their home for several months. In the summer of that year Washington wrote to his old secretary, Tobias Lear: "I am alone at *present*, and shall be glad to see you this evening. Unless some one pops in unexpectedly—Mrs. Washington and myself will do what I believe has not been done within the last twenty Years by us,—that is to set down to dinner by ourselves."

Washington was the soul of hospitality. He enjoyed having people in his house and eating at his board, but there is evidence that toward the last he grew somewhat weary of the stream of strangers. But neither then nor at any other time in his life did he show his impatience to a visitor or turn any man from his door. His patience, was sorely tried at times. For example, we find in his diary under date of September 7, 1785: "At Night, a Man of the name of Purdie, came to offer himself to me as a Housekeeper or Household Steward —he had some testimonials respecting his character—but being intoxicated, and in other respects appearing in an unfavorable light I informed him that he would not answer my purpose, but that he might stay all night."

No matter how many visitors came the Farmer proceeded about his business as usual, particularly in the morning, devoting dinner time and certain hours of the afternoon and evening to those who were sojourning with him. He was obliged, in self-defense, to adopt some such course. He wrote: "My manner of living is plain, and I do not mean to be put out by it. A glass of wine and a bit of mutton are always ready, and such as will be content to partake of them are always welcome. Those who expect more will be disappointed."

After his retirement from the presidency he induced his nephew Lawrence Lewis to come to Mount Vernon and take over some of the duties of entertaining guests, particularly in the evening, as Washington had reached an age when he was averse to staying up late. Lewis not only performed the task satisfactorily, but found incidental diversion that led to matrimony.

Every visitor records that the Farmer was a kind and considerate host. Elkanah Watson relates that one bitter winter night at Mount Vernon, having a severe cold that caused him to cough incessantly, he heard the door of his chamber open gently and there stood the General with a candle in one hand and a bowl of hot tea in another. Doubtless George and Martha had heard the coughing and in family council had decided that their guest must have attention.

Washington was a Cavalier, not a Puritan, and had none of the old New England prejudice against the theater. In fact, it was one of his fondest pleasures from youth to old age. In his Barbadoes journal he records being "treated with a play ticket by Mr. Carter to see the Tragedy of George Barnwell acted." In 1752 he attended a performance at Fredericksburg and thereafter, whenever occasion offered, which during his earlier years was not often, he took advantage of it. He even expressed a desire to act himself. After his resignation and marriage opportunities were more frequent and in his cash memorandum books are many entries of expenditures for tickets to performances at Alexandria and elsewhere. Thus on September 20, 1768, in his daily record of *Where & how my time is Spent* he writes that he "& Mrs. Washington & ye two children were up to Alexandria to see the Inconstant or way to win him acted." Next day he "Stayd in Town all day & saw the Tragedy of Douglas playd."

Such performances were probably given by strolling players who had few accessories in the way of scenery to assist them in creating their illusions.

In September, 1771, when at Annapolis to attend the races, he went to plays four times in five days, the fifth day being Sunday. Two years later, being in New York City, he saw *Hamlet* and *Cross Purposes*.

On many occasions both in this period of his life and later he went to sleight of hand performances, wax works, puppet shows, animal shows, "to hear the Armonica," concerts and other entertainments.

The "association" resolutions of frugality and self-denial by the Continental Congress put an end temporarily to plays in the colonies outside the British lines and put Washington into a greater play, "not, as he once wished, as a performer, but as a character." There were amateur performances at Valley Forge, but they aroused the hostility of the puritanical, and Congress forbade them. Washington seems, however, to have disregarded the interdiction after Yorktown.

He had few opportunities to gratify his fondness for performances in the period of 1784-89, but during his presidency, while residing in New York and Philadelphia, he was a regular attendant. He gave frequent theater parties, sending tickets to his friends. Word that he would attend a play always insured a "full house," and upon his entrance to his box the orchestra would play *Hail Columbia* and *Washington's March* amid great enthusiasm.

The *Federal Gazette* described a performance of *The Maid of the Mill*, which he attended in 1792, as follows:

"When Mr. Hodgkinson as Lord Ainsworth exhibited nobleness of mind in his generosity to the humble miller and his daughter, Patty; when he found her blessed with all the qualities that captivate and endear life, and knew she was capable of adorning a higher sphere; when he had interviews with her upon the subject in which was painted the amiableness of an honorable passion; and after his connection, when he bestowed his benefactions on the relatives, etc., of the old miller, the great and good Washington manifested his approbation of this interesting part of the opera by the tribute of a tear."

Another amusement that both the Farmer and his wife enjoyed greatly was dancing. In his youth he attended balls and "routs" whenever possible and when fighting French and Indians on the frontier he felt as one of his main deprivations his inability to attend the "Assemblies." After his marriage he and his wife went often to balls in Alexandria, attired no doubt in all the bravery of imported English clothes. He describes a ball of 1760 in these terms:

"Went to a ball at Alexandria, where Musick and dancing was the chief entertainment, however, in a convenient room detached for the purpose abounded great plenty of bread and butter, some biscuits, with tea and coffee, which the drinkers of could not distinguish from hot water sweet'ned—Be it remembered that pocket handkerchiefs served the purposes of Table cloths & Napkins and that no apologies were made for either. I shall therefore distinguish this ball by the stile and title of the Bread & Butter Ball."

A certain Mr. Christian conducted a dancing school which met at the homes of the patrons, and the Custis children, John Parke and Martha, were members, as were Elizabeth French of Rose Hill, Milly Posey and others of the neighborhood young people. In 1770 the class met four times at Mount Vernon and we can not doubt that occasionally the host danced with some of the young misses and enjoyed it.

An established institution was the election ball, which took place on the night following the choice of the delegate to the Burgesses. Washington often contributed to the expenses of these balls, particularly when he was himself elected. No doubt they were noisy, hilarious and perhaps now and then a bit rough.

Much has been written of the dances by which Washington and his officers and their ladies helped to while away the tedium of long winters during the Revolution, but the story of these has been often told and besides lies outside the limits of this book, as does the dancing at New York and Philadelphia during his presidency.

There is much conflicting evidence regarding Washington's later dancing exploits. Some writers say that he never tripped the light fantastic after the Revolution and that one of his last participations was at the Fredericksburg ball after the capture of Cornwallis when he "went down some dozen couple in the contra dance." It is certain, however, that long afterward he would at least walk through one or two dances, even though he did not actually take the steps. One good lady who knew him well asserts that he often danced with Nelly Custis, and he seems to have danced in 1796 when he was sixty-four. But to the invitation to the Alexandria assembly early in 1799 he replied:

"Mrs. Washington and myself have been honored with your polite invitation to the assemblies of Alexandria this winter, and thank you for this mark of your attention. But, alas! our dancing days are no more. We wish, however, all those who have a relish for so agreeable and innocent an amusement all the pleasure the season will afford them."

Nor was he puritanical in respect to cards. From his account books we find that he ordered them by the dozen packs, and his diaries contain such entries as "At home all day over cards, it snowing." To increase the interest he not infrequently played for money, though rarely for a large amount. "Loo" and whist seem to have been the games played, but not "bridge" or draw poker, which were then unknown.

From entries in his cash memorandum books it is evident that he loved a quiet game rather frequently. Thus in his memorandum for 1772 I find the entry for September five: "To Cash won at cards" £1.5. Four days later he writes: "To Cash won at Cards at Mrs. Calverts" ten shillings. But on September 17th he lost £1.5; on September 30th, £2, and on October 5th, six shillings. Two days later his luck changed and he won £2.5, while on the seventh he won £12.8. This was the most serious game that I have found a record of, and the cards must either have run well for him or else he had unskilful opponents. The following March, when attending the Burgesses at Williamsburg, he got into a game, probably at Mrs. Campbell's tavern, where he took his meals, and dropped £7.10.

In one of his account books I find two pages devoted to striking a balance between what he won and what he lost from January 7, 1772, to January 1, 1775. In that time he won £72.2.6 and lost £78.5.9. Hence we find the entry: "By balance against Play from Jany. 1772 to this date ... £6.3.3." But he must have had a lot of fun at a cost of that six pounds three shillings and three pence!

It should be remarked here that gaming was then differently regarded in Virginia from what it is now. Many even of the Episcopal clergymen played cards for money and still kept fast hold upon their belief that they would go to Heaven.

The same may also be said of lotteries, in which Washington now and then took a flier. Many of the churches of that day, even in New England, were built partly or wholly with money raised in that way. January 5, 1773, Washington states that he has received sixty tickets in the Delaware lottery from his friend Lord Stirling and that he has "put 12 of the above Sixty into the Hands of the Revd. Mr. Magowan to sell." And "the Revd." sold them too!

In his journal of the trip to Barbadoes taken with his brother Lawrence we find that on his way home he attended "a Great Main of cks [cocks] fought in Yorktown between Gloucester & York for 5 pistoles each battle & 10 ye. odd." Occasionally he seems to have witnessed other mains, but I have found no evidence that he made the practice in any sense a habit.

As a counterweight to his interest in so brutal a sport I must state that he was exceedingly fond of afternoon teas and of the social enjoyments connected with tea drinking. Tea was regularly served at his army headquarters and in summer afternoons on the Mount Vernon veranda.

There is abundant evidence that he also enjoyed horse racing. In September, 1768, he mentions going "to a Purse race at Accotinck," a hamlet a few miles below Mount Vernon where a race track was maintained. In 1772 he attended the Annapolis races, being a guest of the Governor of Maryland, and he repeated the trip in 1773. In the following May he went to a race and barbecue at Johnson's Ferry. George Washington Custis tells us that the Farmer kept blooded horses and that his colt "Magnolia" once ran for a purse, presumably losing, as if the event had been otherwise we should probably have been informed of the fact. In 1786 Washington went to Alexandria "to see the Jockey Club purse run for," and I have noticed a few other references to races, but I conclude that he went less often than some writers would have us believe.

Washington was decidedly an outdoor man. Being six feet two inches tall, and slender rather than heavily made, he was well fitted for athletic sports. Tradition says that he once threw a stone across the Rappahannock at a spot where no other man could do it, and that he could outjump any one in Virginia. He also excelled in the game of putting the bar, as a story related by the artist Peale bears witness.

Of outdoor sports he seems to have enjoyed hunting most. He probably had many unrecorded experiences with deer and turkeys when a surveyor and when in command upon the western border, but his main hunting adventure after big game took place on his trip to the Ohio in 1770. Though the party was on the move most of the time and was looking for rich land rather than for wild animals, they nevertheless took some hunts.

On October twenty-second, in descending the stretch of the Ohio near the mouth of Little Beaver Creek and above the Mingo Town, they saw many wild geese and several kinds of duck and "killed five wild turkeys." Three days later they "saw innumerable quantities of turkeys, and many deer watering and browsing on the shore side, some of which we killed."

He does not say whether they shot this game from the canoe or not, but probably on sighting the game they would put to shore and then one or more would steal up on the quarry. Their success was probably increased by the fact that they had two Indians with them.

Few people are aware of the fact that what is now West Virginia and Ohio then contained many buffaloes. Below the mouth of the Great Hockhocking the voyagers came upon a camp of Indians, the chief of which, an old friend who had accompanied him to warn out the French in 1753, gave Washington "a quarter of very fine buffalo." A creek near the camp, according to the Indians, was an especial resort for these great beasts.

Fourteen miles up the Great Kanawha the travelers took a day off and "went a hunting; killed five buffaloes and wounded some others, three deer, &c. This country abounds in buffaloes and wild game of all kinds; as also in all kinds of wild fowls, there being in the bottoms a great many small grassy ponds, or lakes, which are full of swans, geese, and ducks of different kinds."

How many of the buffaloes fell to his gun Washington does not record, but it is safe to assume that he had at least some shots at them. And beyond question he helped to devour the delicious buffalo humps, these being, with the flesh of the bighorn sheep, the *ne plus ultra* of American big game delicacies.

The region in which these events took place was also notable for its big trees. Near the mouth of the Kanawha they "met with a sycamore about sixty yards from the river of a most extraordinary size, it measuring, three feet from the ground, forty-five feet round [almost fifteen feet through], lacking two inches; and not fifty yards from it was another, thirty-one feet round."

When at home, Washington now and then took a gun and went out after ducks, "hairs," wild turkeys and other game, and occasionally he records fair bags of mallards, teal, bald faces and "blew wings," one of the best being that of February 18, 1768, when he "went a ducking between breakfast and dinner & killed 2 mallards & 5 bald faces." It is doubtful whether he was at all an expert shot. In fact, he much preferred chasing the fox with dogs to hunting with a gun.

Fox hunting in the Virginia of that day was a widely followed sport. It was brought over from England and perhaps its greatest devotee was old Lord Fairfax, with whom Washington hunted when still in his teens. Fairfax, whose seat was at Greenway Court in the Shenandoah Valley, was so passionately fond of it that if foxes were scarce near his home he would go to a locality where they were plentiful, would establish himself at an inn and would keep open house and welcome every person of good character and respectable appearance who cared to join him.

The following are some typical entries from Washington's *Where & how my time is Spent*: "Jany. 1st. (1768) Fox huntg. in my own Neck with Mr. Robt. Alexander and Mr. Colville—catchd nothing—Captn. Posey with us." There were many similar failures and no successes in the next six weeks, but on February twelfth he records joyfully, "Catchd two foxes," and on the thirteenth "catch 2 more foxes." March 2, 1768, "Hunting again, & catchd a fox with a bobd Tail & cut Ears, after 7 hours chase in wch. most of the dogs were worsted." March twenty-ninth, "Fox Hunting with Jacky Custis & Ld. [Lund] Washington—Catchd a fox after 3 hrs. chase." November twenty-second, "Went a fox huntg. with Lord Fairfax & Colo. Fairfax & my Br. Catchd 2 Foxes." For two weeks thereafter they hunted almost every day with varying success. September 30, 1769, he records: "catchd a Rakoon."

On January 27, 1770, the dogs ran a deer out of the Neck and some of them did not get home till next day. The finding of a deer was no uncommon experience, but on no occasion does the chase seem to have been successful, as, when hard pressed, the fugitive would take to the water where the dogs could not follow. January 4, 1772, the hunters "found both a Bear and a Fox but got neither."

Bear and deer were still fairly plentiful in the region, and the fact serves to indicate that the country was not yet thickly settled, nor is it to this day.

In November, 1771, Washington and Jack Custis went to Colonel Mason's at Gunston Hall, a few miles below Mount Vernon, to engage in a grand deer drive in which many men and dogs took part. Mason had an estate of ten thousand acres which was favorably located for such a purpose, being nearly surrounded by water, with peninsulas on which the game could be cornered and forced to take to the river. On the first day they killed two deer, but on the second they killed nothing. No doubt they had a hilarious time of it, dogs baying, horsemen dashing here and there shouting at the top of their voices, and with plenty of fat venison and other good cheer at the Hall that night.

Washington's most remarkable hunting experience occurred on the twenty-third of January, 1770, when he records: "Went a hunting after breakfast & found a Fox at Muddy hole & killed her (it being a Bitch) after a chase of better than two hours & after treeing her twice the last of which times she fell dead out of the Tree after being therein sevl. minutes apparently well." Lest he may be accused of nature faking, it should be explained that the tree was a leaning tree. Occasionally the foxes also took refuge in hollow trees, up which they could climb.

The day usually ended by all the hunters riding to Mount Vernon, Belvoir, Gunston Hall, or some other mansion for a bountiful dinner. Mighty then were the gastronomic feats performed, and over the Madeira the incidents of the day were discussed as Nimrods in all ages are wont to do.

Being so much interested in fox hunting, our Farmer proceeded, with his usual painstaking care, to build up a pack of hounds. The year 1768 was probably the period of his greatest interest in the subject and his diary is full of accounts of the animals. Hounds were now, in fact, his hobby, succeeding in interest his horses. He did his best to breed according to scientific principles, but several entries show that the dogs themselves were inclined blissfully to ignore the laws of eugenics as applied to hounds.

Among his dogs in this period were "Mopsey," "Taster," "Tipler," "Cloe," "Lady," "Forester" and "Captain." August 6, 1768, we learn that "Lady" has four puppies, which are to be called "Vulcan," "Searcher," "Rover," and "Sweetlips."

Like all dog owners he had other troubles with his pets. Once we find him anointing all the hounds that had the mange "with Hogs Lard & Brimstone." Again his pack is menaced by a suspected mad dog, which he shoots.

The Revolution broke rudely in upon the Farmer's sports, but upon his return to Mount Vernon he soon took up the old life. Knowing his bent, Lafayette sent him a pack of French hounds, two dogs and three bitches, and Washington took much interest in them. According to George Washington Custis they were enormous brutes, better built for grappling stags or boars than chasing foxes, and so fierce that a huntsman had to preside at their meals. Their kennel stood a hundred yards south of the old family vault, and Washington visited them every morning and evening. According to Custis, it was the Farmer's desire to have them so evenly matched and trained that if one leading dog should lose the scent, another would be at hand to recover it and thus in full cry you might cover the pack with a blanket.

The biggest of the French hounds, "Vulcan," was so vast that he was often ridden by Master Custis and he seems to have been a rather privileged character. Once when company was expected to dinner Mrs. Washington ordered that a lordly ham should be cooked and served. At dinner she noticed that the ham was not in its place and inquiry developed that "Vulcan" had raided the kitchen and made off with the meat. Thereupon, of course, the mistress scolded and equally, of course, the master smiled and gleefully told the news to the guests.

Billy Lee, the colored valet who had followed the General through the Revolution, usually acted as huntsman and, mounted on "Chinkling" or some other good steed, with a French horn at his back, strove hard to keep the pack in sight, no easy task among the rough timber-covered hills of Fairfax County.

On a hunting day the Farmer breakfasted by candlelight, generally upon corn cakes and milk, and at daybreak, with his guests, Billy and the hounds, sallied forth to find a fox. Washington always rode a good horse and sometimes wore a blue coat, scarlet waistcoat, buckskin breeches, top boots and velvet cap and carried a whip with a long thong. When a fox was started none rode more gallantly or cheered more joyously than did he and as a rule he was in at the death, for, as Jefferson asserts, he was "the best horseman of his age, and the most magnificent figure that could be seen on horseback."

The fox that was generally hunted was the gray fox, which was indigenous to the country. After the Revolution the red fox began to be seen occasionally. They are supposed to have come from the Eastern Shore, and to have crossed Chesapeake Bay on the ice in the hard winter of 1779-80. Custis tells of a famous black fox that would go ten or twenty miles before the hounds and return to the starting-point ready for another run next day. After many unsuccessful chases Billy recommended that the black reynard be let alone, saying he was near akin to another sable and wily character. Thereafter the huntsman was always careful to throw off the hounds when he suspected that they were on the trail of the black fox. This story may or may not be true; all that I can say is that I have found no confirmation of it in Washington's own writings.

Neither have I found there any confirmation of the story that Mrs. Washington and other ladies often rode out to see the hunts. Washington had avenues cut through some of his woods to facilitate the sport and possibly to make the riding easier for the ladies. Upon the whole, however, I incline to the opinion that generally at least Martha stayed at home visiting with lady friends, attending to domestic concerns and superintending the preparation of delectable dishes for the hungry hunters. I very much doubt whether she would have enjoyed seeing a fox killed.

The French hounds were, at least at first, rather indifferent hunters. "Went out after Breakfast with my hounds from France, & two which were lent me, yesterday, by Mr. Mason," says the Farmer the day of the first trial; "found a Fox which was run tolerably well by two of the Frh. Bitches & one of Mason's Dogs—the other French dogs shewed but little disposition to follow —and with the second Dog of Mason's got upon another Fox which was followed slow and indifferently by some & not at all by the rest until the sent became so cold it cd. not be followed at all."

Two days later the dogs failed again and the next time they ran two foxes and caught neither, but their master thought they performed better than hitherto, December 12th:

"After an early breakfast [my nephew] George Washington, Mr. Shaw and Myself went into the Woods back of the Muddy hole Plantation a hunting and were joined by Mr. Lund Washington and Mr. William Peake. About half after ten O'clock (being first plagued with the Dogs running Hogs) we found a fox near Colo Masons Plantation on little Hunting Creek (West fork) having followed on his Drag more than half a Mile; and run him with Eight Dogs (the other 4 getting, as was supposed after a Second Fox) close and well for an hour. When the Dogs came to a fault and to cold Hunting until 20 minutes after when being joined by the missing Dogs they put him up afresh and in about 50 Minutes killed up in an open field of Colo Mason's every Rider & every Dog being present at the Death."

Eight days later the pack chased two foxes, but caught neither. The next hunt is described as follows:

"Went a Fox hunting with the Gentlemen who came here yesterday with Ferdinando Washington and Mr. Shaw, after a very early breakfast.—found a Fox just back of Muddy hole Plantation and after a Chase for an hour and a quarter with my Dogs, & eight couple of Doctor Smiths (brought by Mr. Phil Alexander) we put him into a hollow tree, in which we fastened him, and in the Pincushion put up another Fox which, in an hour and 13 Minutes was killed—We then after allowing the Fox in the hole half an hour put the Dogs upon his Trail & in half a Mile he took to another hollow tree and was again put out of it but he did not go 600 yards before he had recourse to the same shift—finding therefore that he was a conquered Fox we took the Dogs off, and came home to dinner."

Custis asserts that Washington took his last hunt in 1785, but in the diary under date of December 22, 1787, I find that he went out with Major George A. Washington and others on that day, but found

The Flower Garden, By permission of the Mount Vernon Ladies' Association.

nothing, and that he took still another hunt in January, 1788, and chased a fox that had been captured the previous month. This, however, is the last reference that I have discovered. No doubt he was less resilient than in his younger days and found the sport less delightful than of yore, while the duties of the presidency, to which he was soon called, left him little leisure for sport. He seems to have broken up his kennels and to have given away most or all of his hounds.

Later he acquired a pair of "tarriers" and took enough interest in them to write detailed instructions concerning them in 1796.

Washington's fishing was mostly done with a seine as a commercial proposition, but he seems to have had a mild interest in angling. Occasionally he took trips up and down the Potomac in order to fish, sometimes with a hook and line, at other times with seines and nets. He and Doctor Craik took fishing tackle with them on both their western tours and made use of it in some of the mountain streams and also in the Ohio. While at the Federal Convention in 1787 he and Gouverneur Morris went up to Valley Forge partly perhaps to see the old camp, but ostensibly to fish for trout. They lodged at the home of a widow named Moore. On the trip the Farmer learned the Pennsylvania way of raising buckwheat and, it must be confessed, wrote down much more about this topic than about trout. A few days later, with Gouverneur Morris and Mr. and Mrs. Robert Morris, he went up to Trenton and "in the evening fished," with what success he does not relate. When on his eastern tour of 1789 he went outside the harbor of Portsmouth to fish for cod, but the tide was unfavorable and they caught only two. More fortunate was a trip off Sandy Hook the next year, which was thus described by a newspaper:

"Yesterday afternoon the President of the United States returned from Sandy Hook and the fishing banks, where he had been for the benefit of the sea air, and to amuse himself in the delightful recreation of fishing. We are told he has had excellent sport, having himself caught a great number of sea-bass and black fish—the weather proved remarkably fine, which, together with the salubrity of the air and wholesome exercise, rendered this little voyage extremely agreeable."

Our Farmer was extremely fond of fish as an article of diet and took great pains to have them on his table frequently. At Mount Vernon there was an ancient black man, reputed to be a centenarian and the son of an African King, whose duty it was to keep the household supplied with fish. On many a morning he could be seen out on the river in his skiff, beguiling the toothsome perch, bass or rock-fish. Not infrequently he would fall asleep and then the impatient cook, who had orders to have dinner strictly upon the hour, would be compelled to seek the shore and roar at him. Old Jack would waken and upon rowing to shore would inquire angrily: "What you all mek such a debbil of a racket for hey? I wa'nt asleep, only noddin'."

Another colored factotum about the place was known as Tom Davis, whose duty it was to supply the Mansion House with game. With the aid of his old British musket and of his Newfoundland dog "Gunner" he secured many a canvasback and mallard, to say nothing of quails, turkeys and other game.

After the Revolution Washington formed a deer park below the hill on which the Mansion House stands. The park contained about one hundred acres and was surrounded by a high paling about sixteen hundred yards long. At first he had only Virginia deer, but later acquired some English fallow deer from the park of Governor Ogle of Maryland. Both varieties herded together, but never mixed blood. The deer were continually getting out and in February, 1786, one returned with a broken leg, "supposed to be by a shot." Seven years later an English buck that had broken out weeks before was killed by some one. The paddock fence was neglected and ultimately the deer ran half wild over the estate, but in general stayed in the wooded region surrounding the Mansion House. The gardener frequently complained of damage done by them to shrubs and plants, and Washington said he hardly knew "whether to give up the Shrubs or the Deer!" The spring before his death we find him writing to the brothers Chickesters warning them to cease hunting his deer and he hints that he may come to "the disagreeable necessity of resorting to other means."

George Washington Custis, being like his father "Jacky" an enthusiastic hunter, long teased the General to permit him to hunt the deer and at last won consent to shoot one buck. The lad accordingly loaded an old British musket with two ounce-balls, sallied forth and wounded one of the patriarchs of the herd, which was then chased into the Potomac and there slain. Next day the buck was served up to several guests, and Custis long afterward treasured the antlers at Arlington House, the residence he later built across the Potomac from the Federal City.

Upon the whole we must conclude that Washington was one of the best sportsmen of all our Presidents. He was not so much of an Izaak Walton as was one of his successors, nor did he pursue the lion and festive bongo to their African lairs as did another, but he had a keen love of nature and the open country and would have found both the Mighty Hunter and the Mighty Angler kindred spirits.

CHAPTER XV

A CRITICAL VISITOR AT MOUNT VERNON

About thirty miles down the river Potomac, a gentleman, of the name of Grimes, came up to us in his own boat[8]. He had some little time before shot a man who was going across his plantation; and had been tried for so doing, but not punished. He came aboard, and behaved very politely to me: and it being near dinner time, he would have me go ashore and dine with him: which I did. He gave me some grape-juice to drink, which he called Port wine, and entertained me with saying he made it himself: it was not to my taste equal to our Port in England, nor even strong beer; but a hearty welcome makes everything pleasant, and this he most cheerfully gave me. He showed me his garden; the produce of which, he told me, he sold at Alexandria, a distance of thirty miles. His garden was in disorder: and so was everything else I saw about the place; except a favourite stallion, which was in very good condition—a pretty figure of a horse, and of proper size for the road, about fifteen hands high. He likewise showed me some other horses, brood-mares and foals, young colts, &c. of rather an useful kind. His cattle were small, but all much better than the land.

[8] This chapter is taken from *A Tour of America in 1798, 1799, and 1800*, by Richard Parkinson, who has already been several times quoted. Parkinson had won something of a name in England as a scientific agriculturist and had published a book called the *Experienced Farmer*. He negotiated by letter with Washington for the rental of one of the Mount Vernon farms, and in 1798, without having made any definite engagement, sailed for the Potomac with a cargo of good horses, cattle and hogs. His plan for renting Washington's farm fell through, by his account because it was so poor, and ultimately he settled for a time near Baltimore, where he underwent such experiences as an opinionated Englishman with new methods would be likely to meet. Soured by failure, he returned to England, and published an account of his travels, partly with the avowed purpose of discouraging emigration to America. His opinion of the country he summed up thus: "If a man should be so unfortunate as to have married a wife of a capricious disposition, let him take her to America, and keep her there three or four years in a country-place at some distance from a town, and afterwards bring her back to England; if she do not act with propriety, he may be sure there is no remedy." I have rearranged his account in such a way as to make it consecutive, but otherwise it stands as originally published.

He praised the soil very highly. I asked him if he was acquainted with the land at Mount Vernon. He said he was; and represented it to be rich land, but not so rich as his. Yet his I thought very poor indeed; for it was (as is termed in America) *gullied*; which I call broken land. This effect is produced by the winter's frost and summer's rain, which cut the land into cavities of from ten feet wide and ten feet deep (and upwards) in many places; and, added to this, here and there a hole, which makes it look altogether like marlpits, or stone-quarries, that have been carried away by those hasty showers in the summer, which no man who has not seen them in this climate could form any idea of or believe possible....

In two days after we left this place, we came in sight of Mount Vernon; but in all the way up the river, I did not see any green fields. The country had to me a most barren appearance. There were none but snake-fences; which are rails laid with the ends of one upon another, from eight to sixteen in number in one length. The surface of the earth looked like a yellow-washed wall; for it had been a very dry summer; and there was not any thing that I could see green, except the pine trees in the woods, and the cedars, which made a truly picturesque view as we sailed up the Potomac. It is indeed a most beautiful river.

When we arrived at Mount Vernon, I found that General Washington was at Philadelphia; but his steward[9] had orders from the General to receive me and my family, with all the horses, cattle, &c. which I had on board. A boat was, therefore, got ready for landing them; but that could not be done, as the ship must be cleared out at some port before anything was moved: so, after looking about a few minutes at Mount Vernon, I returned to the ship, and we began to make way for Alexandria....

[9] No doubt Anderson, Washington's last manager.

When I had been about seven days at Alexandria, I hired a horse and went to Mount Vernon, to view my intended farm; of which General Washington had given me a plan, and a report along with it—the rent being fixed at eighteen hundred bushels of wheat for twelve hundred acres, or money according to the price of that grain. I must confess that if he would have given me the inheritance of the land for that sum, I durst not have accepted it, especially with the incumbrances upon it; viz. one hundred seventy slaves young and old, and out of that number only twenty-seven[10] in a condition to work, as the steward represented to me. I viewed the whole of the cultivated estate— about three thousand acres; and afterward dined with Mrs. Washington and the family. Here I met a Doctor Thornton, who is a very pleasant agreeable man, and his lady; with a Mr. Peters and his lady, who was a grand-daughter of Mrs. Washington. Doctor Thornton living at the city of Washington, he gave me an invitation to visit him there: he was one of the commissioners of the city.

I slept at Mount Vernon, and experienced a very kind and comfortable reception; but did not like the land at all. I saw no green grass there, except in the garden: and this was some English grass, appearing to me to be a sort of couch-grass; it was in drills. There were also six saintfoin plants, which I found the General valued highly. I viewed the oats which were not thrashed, and counted the grains upon each head; but found no stem with more than four grains, and these a very light and bad quality, such as I had never seen before: the longest straw was of about twelve inches. The wheat was all thrashed, therefore I could not ascertain the produce of that: I saw some of the straw, however, and thought it had been cut and prepared for the cattle in the winter; but I believe I was mistaken, it being short by nature, and with thrashing out looked like chaff, or as if chopped with a bad knife. The General had two thrashing machines, the power given by horses. The clover was very little in bulk, and like chaff; not more than nine inches long, and the leaf very much shed from the stalk. By the stubbles on the land I could not tell which had been wheat, or which had been oats or barley; nor could I see any clover-roots where the clover had grown. The weather was hot and dry at that time; it was in December. The whole of the different fields were covered with either the stalks of weeds, corn-stalks, or what is called sedge—something like spear-grass upon the poor limestone in England; and the steward told me nothing would eat it, which is true. Indeed, he found fault with everything, just like a foreigner; and even told me many unpleasant tales of the General, so that I began to think he feared I was coming to take his place. But (God knows!) I would not choose to accept of it: for he had to superintend four hundred slaves, and there would be more now. This part of his business especially would have been painful to me; it is, in fact, a sort of trade of itself.

I had not in all this time seen what we in England call a corn-stack, nor a dung-hill. There were, indeed, behind the General's barns, two or three cocks of oats and barley; but such as an English broad-wheeled waggon would have carried a hundred miles at one time with ease. Neither had I seen a green plant of any kind: there was some clover of the first year's sowing: but in riding over the fields I should not have known it to be clover, although the steward told me it was; only when I came under a tree I could, by favour of the shade, perceive here and there a green leaf of clover, but I do not remember seeing a green root. I was shown no grass-hay of any kind; nor do I believe there was any.

The cattle were very poor and ordinary, and the sheep the same; nor did I see any thing I liked except the mules, which were very fine ones, and in good condition. Mr. Gough had made a present to General Washington of a bull calf. The animal was shown to me when I first landed at Mount Vernon, and was the first bull I saw in the country. He was large, and very strong-featured; the largest part was his head, the next his legs. The General's steward was a Scotchman, and no judge of animals—a better judge of distilling whiskey.

I saw here a greater number of negroes than I ever saw at one time, either before or since.

The house is a very decent mansion: not large, and something like a gentleman's house in England, with gardens and plantations; and is very prettily situated on the banks of the river Potowmac, with extensive prospects.... The roads are very bad from Alexandria to Mount Vernon.

The General still continuing at Philadelphia, I could not have the pleasure of seeing him; therefore I returned to Alexandria.

I returned [to Mount Vernon some weeks later] ... to see General Washington. I dined with him; and he showed me several presents that had been sent him, viz. swords, china, and among the rest the key of the Bastille. I spent a very pleasant day in the house, as the weather was so severe that there were no farming objects to see, the ground being covered with snow.

Would General Washington have given me the twelve hundred acres I would not have accepted it, to have been confined to live in that country; and to convince the General of the cause of my determination, I was compelled to treat him with a great deal of frankness. The General, who had corresponded with Mr. Arthur Young and others on the subject of English farming and soils, and had been not a little flattered by different gentlemen from England, seemed at first to be not well pleased with my conversation; but I gave him some strong proofs of his mistakes, by making a comparison between the lands in America and those of England in two respects.

First, in the article of sheep. He supposed himself to have fine sheep, and a great quantity of them. At the time of my viewing his five farms, which consisted of about three thousand acres cultivated, he had one hundred sheep, and those in very poor condition. This was in the month of November. To show him his mistake in the value and quality of his land, I compared this with the farm my father occupied, which was less than six hundred acres. He clipped eleven hundred sheep, though some of his land was poor and at two shillings and sixpence per acre—the highest was at twenty shillings; the average weight of the wool was ten pounds per fleece, and the carcases weighed from eighty to one hundred twenty pounds each: while in the General's hundred sheep on three thousand acres, the wool would not weigh on an average more than three pounds and a half the fleece, and the carcases at forty-eight pounds each. Secondly, the proportion of the produce in grain was similar. The General's crops were from two to three[11] bushels of wheat per acre; and my father's farm, although poor clay soil, gave from twenty to thirty bushels.

[11] A misstatement, of course.

During this conversation Colonel Lear, aide-de-camp to the General, was present. When the General left the room, the Colonel told me he had himself been in England, and had seen Arthur Young (who had been frequently named by the General in our conversation); and that Mr. Young having learnt that he was in the mercantile line, and was possessed of much land, had said he thought he was a great fool to be a merchant and yet have so much land; the Colonel replied, that if Mr. Young had the same land to cultivate, it would make a great fool of *him*. The Colonel did me the honour to say I was the only man he ever knew to treat General Washington with frankness.

The General's cattle at that time were all in poor condition: except his mules (bred from American mares), which were very fine, and the Spanish ass sent to him as a present by the king of Spain. I felt myself much vexed at an expression used at dinner by Mrs. Washington. When the General and the company at table were talking about the fine horses and cattle I had brought from England, Mrs. Washington said, "I am afraid, Mr. Parkinson, you have brought your fine horses and cattle to a bad market; I am of opinion that our horses and cattle are good enough for our land." I thought that if every old woman in the country knew this, my speculation would answer very ill: as I perfectly agreed with Mrs. Washington in sentiment; and wondered much, from the poverty of the land, to see the cattle good as they were.

The General wished me to stay all night; but having some other engagement, I declined his kind offer. He sent Colonel Lear out after I had parted with him, to ask me if I wanted any money; which I gladly accepted.

CHAPTER XVI

PROFIT AND LOSS

A biographer whose opinions about Washington are usually sound concludes that the General was a failure as a farmer. With this opinion I am unable to agree and I am inclined to think that in forming it he had in mind temporary financial stringencies and perhaps a comparison between Washington and the scientific farmers of to-day instead of the juster comparison with the farmers of that day. For if Washington was a failure, then nine-tenths of the Southern planters of his day were also failures, for their methods and results were much worse than his.

It must be admitted, however, that comparatively little of his fortune, which amounted at his death to perhaps three-quarters of a million dollars, was made by the sale of products from his farm. Few farmers have grown rich in that way. Washington's wealth was due in part to inheritance and a fortunate marriage, but most of all to the increment on land. Part of this land he received as a reward for military services, but much of it he was shrewd enough to buy at a low rate and hold until it became more valuable.

The task of analyzing his fortune and income in detail is an impossible one for a number of reasons. We do not have all the facts of his financial operations and even if we had there are other difficulties. A farmer, unlike a salaried man, can not tell with any exactness what his true income is. The salaried man can say, "This year I received four thousand dollars," The farmer can only say—if he is the one in a hundred who keeps accounts—"Last year I took in two thousand dollars or five thousand dollars," as the case may be. From this sum he must deduct expenses for labor, wear and tear of farm machinery, pro rata cost of new tools and machinery, loss of soil fertility, must take into account the fact that some of the stock sold has been growing for one, two or more years, must allow for the butter and eggs bartered for groceries and for the value of the two cows he traded for a horse, must add the value of the rent of the house and grounds he and his family have enjoyed, the value of the chickens, eggs, vegetables, fruit, milk, meat and other produce of the farm consumed—as he proceeds the problem becomes infinitely more complex until at last he gives it up as hopeless.

This much, however, is plain—a farmer can handle much less money than a salaried man and yet live infinitely better, for his rent, much of his food and many other things cost him nothing.

In Washington's case the problem is further complicated by a number of circumstances. As a result of his marriage he had some money upon bond. For his military services in the French war he received large grants of land and the payment during the Revolution of his personal expenses, and as President he had a salary of twenty-five thousand dollars a year.

Yet another difficulty discloses itself when we come to examine his cash accounts. We find, for example, that from August 3, 1775, to September, 1783, leaving out of the reckoning his military receipts, he took in a total of about eighty thousand one hundred sixty-seven pounds. What then more simple than to divide this sum by seven and ascertain his average receipts during the years of the Revolution? But when we come to examine some of the details more closely we are brought to pause. We discover such facts as that in 1780 a small steer, supposed to weigh about three hundred pounds, brought five hundred pounds in money! A sheep sold for one hundred pounds; six thousand five hundred sixty-nine pounds of dressed beef brought six thousand five hundred sixty-nine pounds; the stud fee for "Steady" was sixty pounds. In other words, the accounts in these years were in depreciated paper and utterly worthless for our purposes. Washington himself gave the puzzle up in despair toward the end of the war and paid his manager in produce, not money.

We of to-day have, in fact, not the faintest conception of the blessing we enjoy in a uniform and fairly stable monetary system. Even before the days of the "Continentals" there was depreciated paper afloat that had been issued by the colonial governments and, unless the fact is definitely stated, when we come upon figures of that period we can never be sure whether they refer to pounds sterling or pounds paper, or, if the latter, what kind of paper. People had to be constantly figuring the real value of Pennsylvania money, or Virginia money or Massachusetts money, and one meets with many such calculations on the blank leaves of Washington's account books. Even metallic money was a Chinese puzzle except to the initiated, there were so many kinds of it afloat. Among our Farmer's papers I have found a list of the money that he took with him to Philadelphia on one occasion—6 joes, 67 half joes, 2 one-eighteenth joes, 3 doubloons, 1 pistole, 2 moidores, 1 half moidore, 2 double louis d'or, 3 single louis d'or, 80 guineas, 7 half guineas, besides silver and bank-notes.

The depreciation of the paper currency during the Revolution proved disastrous to him in several ways. When the war broke out much of the money he had obtained by marriage was loaned out on bond, or, as we would say to-day, on mortgage. "I am now receiving," he soon wrote, "a shilling in the pound in discharge of Bonds which ought to have been paid me, & would have been realized before I left Virginia, but for my indulgences to the debtors." In 1778 he said that six or seven thousand pounds that he had in bonds upon interest had been paid in depreciated paper, so that the real value was now reduced to as many hundreds. Some of the paper money that came into his hands he invested in government securities, and at least ten thousand pounds of these in Virginia money were ultimately funded by the federal government for six thousand two hundred and forty-six dollars in three and six per cent. bonds.

And yet, by examining Washington's accounts, one is able to estimate in a rough way the returns he received from his estate, landed and otherwise. We find that in ten months of 1759 he took in £1,839; from January 1, 1760, to January 10, 1761, about £2,535; in 1772, £3,213; from August 3, 1775, to August 30, 1776, £2,119; in 1786, £2,025; in 1791, about £2,025. Included in some of these entries, particularly the earlier ones, are payments of interest and principal on his wife's share of the Custis estate. Of the later ones, that for 1786—a bad farming year—includes rentals on more than a score of parcels of land amounting to £282.15, £25 rental on his fishery, payments for flour, stud fees, etc.

Upon the average, therefore, I am inclined to believe that his annual receipts were roughly in the neighborhood of ten thousand dollars to fifteen thousand dollars a year from his estate.

As regards Mount Vernon alone, he sometimes made estimates of what the crop returns ought to

A Page from a Cash Memorandum Book.

be; in other words, counted his chickens before they were hatched. Thus in

1789 he drew up alternative plans and estimated that one of these, if adopted, ought to produce crops worth a gross of £3,091, another £3,831, and a third £4,449, but that from these sums £1,357, £1,394 and £1,445 respectively would have to be deducted for seed, food for man and beasts, and other expenses.

A much better idea of the financial returns from his home estate can be obtained from his actual balances of gain and loss. One of these, namely for 1798, which was a poor year, was as follows:

```
        BALANCE OF GAIN AND LOSS, 1798

  DR. GAINED                     CR. LOST

  Dogue Run Farm   397.11.2      Mansion House .. 466.18. 2-
  1/2
  Union Farm …. 529.10.11-1/2    Muddy Hole Farm   60. 1. 3-1/2
  River Farm …. 234. 4.11        Spinning ……. 51. 2.  0
  Smith's Shop .. 34.12.09-1/2     Hire of Head
  Distillery …. 83.13. 1          overseer ….. 140. 0. 0
  Jacks ……… 56.1
  Traveler …… 9.17
    (stud horse)
  Shoemaker ….. 28.17. 1
  Fishery ……. 165.12. 0-1/4    By clear gain on
  Dairy ……… 30.12. 3          the Estate…..£898.16. 4-1/4
```

Mr. Paul Leicester Ford considered this "a pretty poor showing for an estate and negroes which had certainly cost him over fifty thousand dollars, and on which there was live stock which at the lowest estimation was worth fifteen thousand dollars more." In some respects it was a poor showing. Yet the profit Washington sets down is about seven per cent. upon sixty-five thousand dollars, and seven per cent. is more than the average farmer makes off his farm to-day except through the appreciation in the value of the land. The truth is, however, that Mount Vernon, including the live stock and slaves, was really worth in 1798 nearer two hundred thousand dollars than sixty-five thousand, so that the actual return would only be about two and a fourth per cent.

But Washington failed to include in his receipts many items, such as the use of a fine mansion for himself and family, the use of horses and vehicles, and the added value of slaves and live stock by natural increase.

Besides in some other years the profits were much larger.

And lastly, in judging a man's success or failure as a farmer, allowance must be made for the kind of land that he has to farm. The Mount Vernon land was undoubtedly poor in quality, and it is probable that Washington got more out of it than has ever been got out of it by any other person either before or since. Much of it to-day must not pay taxes.

Washington died possessed of property worth about three-quarters of a million, although he began life glad to earn a doubloon a day surveying. The main sources of this wealth have already been indicated, but when all allowance is made in these respects, the fact remains that he was compelled to make a living and to keep expenses paid during the forty years in which the fortune was accumulating, and the main source he drew from was his farms. Not much of that living came from the Custis estate, for, as we have seen, a large part of the money thus acquired was lost. During his eight years as Commander-in-Chief he had his expenses—no more. Of the eight years of his presidency much the same can be said, for all authorities agree that he expended all of his salary in maintaining his position and some say that he spent more. Yet at the end of his life we find him with much more land than he had in 1760, with valuable stocks and bonds, a house and furniture infinitely superior to the eight-room house he first owned, two houses in the Federal City that had cost him about $15,000, several times as many negroes, and live stock estimated by himself at $15,653 and by his manager at upward of twice that sum.

Such being the case—and as no one has ever ventured even to hint that he made money corruptly out of his official position—the conclusion is irresistible that he was a good business man and that he made farming pay, particularly when he was at home.

It is true that only three months before his death he wrote: "The expense at which I live, and the unproductiveness of my estate, will not allow me to lessen my income while I remain in my present situation. On the contrary, were it not for occasional supplies of money in payment for lands sold within the last four or five years, to the amount of upwards of fifty thousand dollars, I should not be able to support the former without involving myself in debt and difficulties," This must be taken, however, to apply to a single period of heavy expense when foreign complications and other causes rendered farming unprofitable, rather than to his whole career. Furthermore, his landed investments from which he could draw no returns were so heavy that he had approached the condition of being land poor and it was only proper that he should cut loose from some of them.

CHAPTER XVII

ODDS AND ENDS

In an age when organized charity was almost unknown the burden of such work fell mainly upon individuals. Being a man of great prominence and known to be wealthy, the proprietor of Mount Vernon was the recipient of many requests for assistance. Ministers wrote to beg money to rebuild churches or to convert the heathen; old soldiers wrote to ask for money to relieve family distresses or to use in business; from all classes and sections poured in requests for aid, financial and otherwise.

It was inevitable that among these requests there should be some that were unusual. Perhaps the most amusing that I have discovered is one written by a young man named Thomas Bruff, from the Fountain Inn, Georgetown. He states that this is his second letter, but I have not found the first. In the letter we have he sets forth that he has lost all his property and desires a loan of five hundred pounds. His need is urgent, for he is engaged to a beautiful and "amiable" young lady, possessed of an "Estate that will render me Independent. Whom I cannot Marry in my present situation.... All my Happyness is now depending upon your Goodness and without your kind assistance I must be forever miserable—I should have never thought of making application to you for this favor had it not been in Consequence of a vision by Night since my Fathers Death who appeared to me in a Dream in my Misfortunes three times in one Night telling me to make applycation to you for Money and that you would relieve me from my distresses. He appeared the other night again and asked me if I had obeyed his commands I informed him that I had Wrote to you some time ago but had Received no answer nor no information Relative to the Business he then observed that he expected my letter had not come to hand and toald me to Write again I made some Objections at first and toald him I thought it presumption in me to trouble your Excellency again on the subject he then in a Rage drew his Small Sword and toald me if I did not he would run me through. I immediately in a fright consented."

One might suppose that so ingenious a request, picturing the deadly danger in which a young man stood from the shade of his progenitor, especially a young man who was thereby forced to keep a young lady waiting, would have aroused Washington's most generous impulses and caused him to send perhaps double the amount desired. Possibly he was hard up at the time. At all events he indorsed the letter thus:

"Without date and without success."

Many times, however, our Farmer was open-handed to persons who had no personal claim on him. For example, he loaned three hundred and two pounds to his old comrade of the French War—Robert Stewart—the purpose being to buy a commission in the British army. So far as I can discover it was never repaid; in fact, I am not sure but that he intended it as a gift. Another advance was that made to Charles L. Carter, probably the young man who later married a daughter of Washington's sister, Betty Lewis. Most of the story is told in the following extract from a letter written by Carter from Fredericksburg, June 2, 1797:

"With diffidence I now address you in consequence of having failed after my first voyage from China, to return the two hundred Dollars you favored me with the Loan of. Be assured Dr. Sir that I left goods unsold at the time of my Departure from Philadelphia on the second voyage, & directed that the money arising therefrom should be paid to you, but the integrity of my agent did not prove to be so uncorrupted as I had flattered myself. I have, at this late period, sent by Mr. G. Tevis the sum of two hundred Dollars with interest therefrom from the 15th of March 1795 to the 1st June, 1797. That sum has laid the foundation of a pretty fortune, for which I shall ever feel myself indebted to you."

He added that he had been refused the loan by a near relation before Washington had so kindly obliged him and that his mother, who was evidently acquainted with Washington, joined in hearty thanks for the benefit received.

Washington had experienced enough instances of ingratitude to be much pleased with the outcome of this affair. He replied in the kindest terms, but declined to receive the interest, saying that he had not made the loan as an investment and that he did not desire a profit from it.

Another recipient of Washington's bounty was his old neighbor, Captain John Posey. Posey sold Washington not only his Ferry Farm but also his claim to western lands. He became financially embarrassed, in fact, ruined; his family was scattered, and he made frequent applications to Washington for advice and assistance. Washington helped to educate a son, St. Lawrence, who had been reduced to the hard expedient of tending bar in a tavern, and he also kept a daughter, Milly, at Mount Vernon, perhaps as a sort of companion to Mrs. Washington. The Captain once wrote:

"I could [have] been able to [have] Satisfied all my old Arrears, some months AGoe, by marrying [an] old widow woman in this County. She has large soms

[of] cash by her, and Prittey good Est.—She is as thick as she is high—And gits drunk at Least three or foure [times] a weak—which is Disagreable to me —has Viliant Sperrit when Drunk—its been [a] great Dispute in my mind what to Doe,—I beleave I shu'd Run all Resks—if my Last wife, had been [an] Even temper'd woman, but her Sperrit, has Given me such [a] Shock— that I am afraid to Run the Resk again."

Evidently the Captain did not find a way out of his troubles by the matrimonial route, for somewhat later he was in jail at Queenstown, presumably for debt, and we find in one of Washington's cash memorandum books under date of October 15, 1773: "By Charity—given Captn. Posey," four pounds. One of the sons later settled in Indiana, and the "Pocket" county is named after him.

Another boy toward whose education Washington contributed was the son of Doctor James Craik—the boy being a namesake. Doctor Craik was one of Washington's oldest and dearest friends. He was born in Scotland two years before Washington saw the light at Wakefield, graduated from Edinburgh University, practised medicine in the West Indies for a short time and then came to Virginia. He was Washington's comrade in arms in the Fort Necessity campaign, was subsequently surgeon general in the Continental Army, and accompanied Washington to the Ohio both in 1770 and 1784. He married Mariane Ewell, a relative of Washington's mother, and resided many years in Alexandria. He was a frequent visitor at Mount Vernon both as a friend and in a professional capacity, and Washington declared that he would rather trust him than a dozen other doctors. Few men were so close to the great man as he, and he was one of the few who in his letters ventured to tell chatty matters of gossip. Thus, in August, 1791, he wrote a letter apropos of the bad health of George A. Washington and added: "My daughter Nancy is there [Mt. Vernon] by way of Amusement awhile. She begins to be tired of her Fathers house and I believe intends taking an old Batchelor Mr. Hn. for a mate shortly." Another young lady, Miss Muir, who had recently gone to Long Island for the benefit of the sea baths was "pursued" by a Mr. Donaldson and the latter now writes that "he shall bring back a wife with him." Craik was a thorough believer in Washington's destiny, and in the dark days of the Revolution would hearten up his comrades by the story of the Indian chieftain met upon the Ohio in 1770 who had vainly tried to kill Washington in the battle of the Monongahela and had finally desisted in the belief that he was invulnerable.

To friends, family, church, education and strangers our Farmer was open-handed beyond most men of his time. His manager had orders to fill a corn-house every year for the sole use of the poor in the neighborhood and this saved numbers of poor women and children from extreme want. He also allowed the honest poor to make use of his fishing stations, furnishing them with all necessary apparatus for taking herring, and if they were unequal to the task of hauling the seine, assistance was rendered them by the General's servants.

To Lund Washington he wrote from the camp at Cambridge: "Let the hospitality of the house, with respect to the poor, be kept up. Let no one go hungry away. If any of this kind of people should be in want of corn, supply their necessaries, provided that it does not encourage them to idleness; and I have no objection to you giving my money in charity to the amount of forty or fifty pounds a year, when you think it well bestowed. What I mean by having no objection is, that it is my desire it should be done. You are to consider that neither *myself nor wife* is now in the way to do these good offices."

His relations with his own kindred were patriarchal in character. His care of Mrs. Washington's children and grandchildren has already been described. He gave a phaeton and money to the extent of two thousand five hundred dollars to his mother and did not claim possession of some of the land left him by his father's will. To his sister Betty Lewis he gave a mule and many other presents, as well as employment to several of her sons. He loaned his brother Samuel (five times married) considerable sums, which he forgave in his will, spent "near five thousand dollars" on the education of two of his sons, and cared for several years for a daughter Harriot, notwithstanding the fact that she had "no disposition ... to be careful of her cloaths." To his nephew, Bushrod Washington, he gave money and helped him to obtain a legal education, and he assisted another nephew, George A. Washington, and his widow and children, in ways already mentioned. Over forty relatives were remembered in his will, many of them in a most substantial manner.

In the matter of eating and drinking Washington was abstemious. For breakfast he ordinarily had tea and Indian cakes with butter and perhaps honey, of which he was very fond. His supper was equally light, consisting of perhaps tea and toast, with wine, and he usually retired promptly at nine o'clock. Dinner was the main meal of the day at Mount Vernon, and was served punctually at two o'clock. One such meal is thus described by a guest:

"He thanked us, desired us to be seated, and to excuse him a few moments.... The President came and desired us to walk in to dinner and directed us where to sit, (no grace was said).... The dinner was very good, a small roasted pigg, boiled leg of lamb, roasted fowls, beef, peas, lettice, cucumbers, artichokes, etc., puddings, tarts, etc. etc. We were desired to call for what drink we chose. He took a glass of wine with Mrs. Law first, which example was followed by Dr. Croker Crakes and Mrs. Washington, myself and Mrs. Peters, Mr. Fayette and the young lady whose name is Custis. When the cloth was taken away the President gave 'all our Friends.'"

The General ordinarily confined himself to a few courses and if offered anything very rich would reply, "That is too good for me." He often drank beer with the meal, with one or two glasses of wine and perhaps as many more afterward, often eating nuts, another delicacy with him, as he sipped the wine.

He was, in fact, no prohibitionist, but he was a strong believer in temperance. He and the public men of his time, being aristocrats, were wine drinkers and few of them were drunkards. The political revolution of 1830, ushered in by Jackson, brought in a different type—Westerners who drank whisky and brandy, with the result that drunkenness in public

One of Washington's Tavern Bills.

station was much more common. Many of the Virginia gentlemen of Washington's day spent a fourth or even a third of their income upon their cellars. He was no exception to the rule, and from his papers we discover many purchases of wine. One of the last bills of lading I have noticed among his papers is a bill for "Two pipes of fine old London particular Madeira Wine," shipped to him from the island of Madeira, September 20, 1799. One wonders whether he got to toast "All our Friends" out of it before he died.

His sideboard and table were well equipped with glasses and silver wine coolers of the most expensive construction. As in many other matters, his inventive bent turned in this direction. Having noticed the confusion that often arose from the passing of the bottles about the table he designed when President a sort of silver caster capable of holding four bottles. They were used with great success on state occasions and were so convenient that other people adopted the invention, so that wine *coasters*, after the Washington design, became a part of the furniture of every fashionable sideboard.

To cool wine, meat and other articles, Washington early adopted the practice of putting up ice, a thing then unusual. In January, 1785, he prepared a dry well under the summer house and also one in his new cellar and in due time had both filled. June fifth he "Opened the well in my Cellar in which I had laid up a store of Ice, but there was not the smallest particle remaining.—I then opened the other Repository (call the dry Well) in which I found a large store." Later he erected an ice house to the eastward of the flower garden.

His experience with the cellar well was hardly less successful than that of his friend, James Madison, on a like occasion. Madison had an ice house filled with ice, and a skeptical overseer wagered a turkey against a mint julep that by the fourth of July the ice would all have disappeared. The day came, they opened the house, and behold there was enough ice for exactly *one* julep! Truly a sad situation when there were *two* Virginia gentlemen.

Mention of Madison in this connection calls to mind the popular notion that it was his wife Dolly who invented ice-cream. I believe that her biographers claim for her the credit of the discovery. The rôle of the iconoclast is a thankless one and I confess to a liking for Dolly, but I have discovered in Washington's cash memorandum book under date of May 17, 1784, the entry: "By a Cream Machine for Ice," £1.13.4—that is an ice-cream freezer. The immortal Dolly was then not quite twelve years old.

Washington seems to have owned three coaches. The first he ordered in London in 1758 in preparation for his marriage. It was to be fashionable, genteel and of seasoned wood; the body preferably green, with a light gilding on the mouldings, with other suitable ornaments including the Washington arms. It was sent with high recommendations, but proved to be of badly seasoned material, so that the panels shrunk and slipped out of the mouldings within two months and split from end to end, much to his disgust. Such a chariot was driven not with lines from a driver's box, but by liveried postillions riding on horseback, one horseman to each span.

The second coach he had made in Philadelphia in 1780 at a cost of two hundred and ten pounds in specie. It was decidedly better built.

The last was a coach, called "the White Chariot," bought second hand soon after he became President. It was built by Clarke, of Philadelphia, and was a fine vehicle, with a cream-colored body and wheels, green Venetian blinds and the Washington arms painted upon the doors. In this coach, drawn by six horses, he drove out in state at Philadelphia and rode to and from Mount Vernon, occasionally suffering an upset on the wretched roads. It was strong and of good workmanship and its maker heard with pride that it had made the long southern tour of 1791 without starting a nail or a screw. This coach was purchased at the sale of the General's effects by George Washington Parke Custis and later in a curious manner fell into the possession of BishopMeade, who ultimately made it up into walking sticks, picture frames, snuff boxes and such mementoes.

At Mount Vernon to-day the visitor is shown a coach which the official Handbook states is vouched for as the original "White Chariot." In reality it seems to be the coach once owned by the Powell family of Philadelphia. It is said to have been built by the same maker and on the same lines, and Washington may have ridden in it, but it never belonged to him.

Most people think of Washington as a marble statue on a pedestal rather than as a being of flesh and blood with human feelings, faults and virtues. He was self-contained, he was not voluble, he had a sense of personal dignity, but underneath he was not cold. He was really hot-tempered and on a few well-authenticated occasions fell into passions in which he used language that would have blistered the steel sides of a dreadnaught. Yet he was kind-hearted, he pitied the weak and sorrowful, and the list of his quiet benefactions would fill many pages and cost him thousands of pounds. He was even full of sentiment in some matters; on more than one occasion he provided positions that enabled young friends or relatives to marry, and I shrewdly suspect that he engineered matters so that the beloved Nelly Custis obtained a good husband in the person of his nephew, Lawrence Lewis. I might say much more tending to show his human qualities, but I shall add only this: Having for many years studied his career from every imaginable point of view, I give it as my deliberate opinion that perhaps no man ever lived who was more considerate of the rights and feelings of others. Not even Lincoln had a bigger heart.

CHAPTER XVIII

THE VALE OF SUNSET

Washington looked forward to the end of his presidency as does "the weariest traveler, who sees a resting-place, and is bending his body to lay thereon." "Methought I heard him say, 'Ay.' I am fairly out, and you are fairly in; see which of us is the happiest," wrote John Adams to his wife Abigail. And from Mount Vernon Nelly Custis informed a friend that "grandpapa is very well and much pleased with being once more Farmer Washington."

The eight years of toilsome work, which had been rendered all the harder by much bitter criticism, had aged him greatly and this helped to make him doubly anxious to return to the peace and quiet of home for his final days. And yet he was affected by his parting from his friends and associates. A few partisan enemies openly rejoiced at his departure, but there were not wanting abundant evidences of the people's reverence and love for him. It is a source of satisfaction to us now that his contemporaries realized he was one of the great figures of history and that they did not withhold the tribute of their praise until after his death. As we turn the thousands of manuscripts that make up his papers we come upon scores of private letters and public resolutions in which, in terms often a bit stilted but none the less sincere, a country's gratitude is laid at the feet of its benefactor.

The Mount Vernon to which he returned was perhaps in better condition than was that to which he retired at the end of the Revolution, for he had been able each summer to give the estate some personal oversight; nevertheless it was badly run down and there was much to occupy his attention. In April he wrote: "We are in the midst of litter and dirt, occasioned by joiners, masons, painters, and upholsterers, working in the house, all parts of which, as well as the outbuildings, are much out of repair."

Anderson remained with him, but Washington gave personal attention to many matters and exercised a general oversight over everything. Like most good farmers he "began his diurnal course with the sun," and if his slaves and hirelings were not in place by that time he sent "them messages of sorrow for their indisposition." Having set the wheels of the estate in motion, he breakfasted. "This being over, I mount my horse and ride around my farms, which employs me until it is time for dinner, at which I rarely miss seeing strange faces.... The usual time of sitting at table, a walk, and tea bring me within the dawn of candlelight; previous to which, if not prevented by company, I resolve that, as soon as the glimmering taper supplies the place of the great luminary, I will retire to my writing table and acknowledge the letters I have received, but when the lights are brought I feel tired and disinclined to engage in this work, conceiving that the next night will do as well. The next night comes, and with it the same causes of postponement, and so on.... I have not looked into a book since I came home; nor shall I be able to do it until I have discharged my workmen, probably not before the nights grow longer, when possibly I may be looking in Doomsday Book."

He had his usual troubles with servants and crops, with delinquent tenants and other debtors; he tried Booker's threshing machine, experimented with white Indian peas and several varieties of wheat, including a yellow bearded kind that was supposed to resist the fly, and built two houses, or rather a double house, on property owned in the Federal City—he avoided calling the place "Washington."

A picture of the Farmer out upon his rounds in these last days has been left us by his adopted son, George Washington Parke Custis. Custis relates that one day when out with a gun he met on the forest road an elderly gentleman on horseback who inquired where he could find the General. The boy told the stranger, who proved to be Colonel Meade, once of Washington's staff, that the General was abroad on the estate and pointed out what direction to take to come upon him. "You will meet, sir, with an old gentleman riding alone in plain drab clothes, a broad-brimmed white hat, a hickory switch in his hand, and carrying an umbrella with a long staff, which is attached to his saddle-bow—that person, sir, is General Washington."

Those were pleasant rides the old Farmer took in the early morning sunshine, with the birds singing about him, the dirt lanes soft under his horse's feet, and in his nostrils the pure air fragrant with the scent of pines, locust blossoms or wild honeysuckle. When he grew thirsty he would pause for a drink at his favorite gum spring, and as he made his rounds would note the progress of the miller, the coopers, the carpenters, the fishermen, and the hands in the fields, how the corn was coming up or the wheat was ripening, what fences needed to be renewed or gaps in hedges filled, what the increase of his cattle would be, whether the stand of clover or buckwheat was good or not. He was the owner of all this great estate, he was proud of it; it was his home, and he was glad to be back on it once more. For he had long since realized that there are deeper and more satisfying pleasures than winning battles or enjoying the plaudits of multitudes.

An English actor named John Bernard who happened to be in Virginia in this period has left us a delightfully intimate picture of the Farmer on his rounds.

Bernard had ridden out below Alexandria to pay a visit and on his return came upon an overturned chaise containing a man and a woman. About the same time another horseman rode up from the opposite direction. The two quickly ascertained that the man was unhurt and managed to restore the wife to consciousness, whereupon she began to upbraid her husband for carelessness.

"The horse," continues Bernard, "was now on his legs, but the vehicle was still prostrate, heavy in its frame and laden with at least half a ton of luggage. My fellow-helper set me an example of activity in relieving it of internal weight; and when all was clear we grasped the wheel between us and to the peril of our spinal columns righted the conveyance. The horse was then put in and we lent a hand to help up the luggage. All this helping, hauling and lifting occupied at least half an hour under a meridian sun, in the middle of July, which fairly boiled the perspiration out of our foreheads."

After the two Samaritans had declined a pressing invitation to go to Alexandria and have a drop of something, the unknown, a tall man past middle age, wearing a blue coat and buckskin breeches, exclaimed impatiently at the heat and then "offered very courteously," says Bernard, "to dust my coat, a favor the return of which enabled me to take a deliberate survey of his person."

The stranger then called Bernard by name, saying that he had seen him play in Philadelphia, and asked him to accompany him to his house and rest, at the same time pointing out a mansion on a distant hill. Not till then did Bernard realize with whom he was speaking.

"Mt. Vernon!" he exclaimed. "Have I the honor of addressing General Washington?"

With a smile Washington extended his hand and said: "An odd sort of introduction, Mr. Bernard; but I am pleased to find that you can play so active a part in private and without a prompter."

Then they rode up to the Mansion House and had a pleasant chat[12].

[12] This anecdote is accepted by Mr. Lodge in his life of Washington, but doubt is cast upon it by another historian. All that can be said is that there is nothing to disprove it and that it is not inherently improbable.

Upon his retirement from the presidency our Farmer had told Oliver Wolcott that he probably would never again go twenty miles from his own vine and fig tree, but the troubles with France resulted in a quasi-war and he was once more called from retirement to head an army, most of which was never raised. He accepted the appointment with the understanding that he was not to be called into the field unless his presence should be indispensable, but he found that he must give much of his time to the matter and be often from home, while a quarrel between his friends Knox and Hamilton over second place joined with Republican hostility to war measures to add a touch of bitterness to the work. Happily war was avoided and, though an adjustment of the international difficulties was not reached until 1800, Washington was able to spend most of the last months of his life at Mount Vernon comparatively undisturbed.

Yet things were not as once they were. Mrs. Washington had aged greatly and was now a semi-invalid often confined to her bed. The Farmer himself came of short-lived stock and realized that his pilgrimage would not be greatly prolonged. Twice during the year he was seriously ill, and in September was laid up for more than a week. His brother Charles died and in acknowledging the sad news he wrote:

"I was the first, and am, now, the last of my father's children by the second marriage, who remain.

"When I shall be *called upon to follow them* is known only to the Giver of Life. When the summons comes, I shall endeavor to obey it with good grace."

And yet there were gleams of joy and gladness. "About candlelight" on his birthday in 1799 Nelly Custis and his nephew, Lawrence Lewis, were wedded. The bride wished him to wear his gorgeous new uniform, but when he came down to give her away he wore the old Continental buff and blue and no doubt all loved him better so. Often thereafter the pair were at Mount Vernon and there on November twenty-seventh a little daughter came as the first pledge of their affection. As always there was much company. In August came a gallant kinsman from South Carolina, once Colonel but now General William Washington of Cowpens fame, and for three days the house was filled with guests and there was feasting and visiting. November fifteenth Washington "Rode to visit Mr. now Lord Fairfax," who was back from England with his family, and the renewal of old friendships proved so agreeable that in the next month the families dined back and forth repeatedly.

Nor did the Farmer cease to labor or to lay plans for the future. He entered into negotiations for the purchase of more land to round out Mount Vernon and surveyed some tracts that he owned. On the tenth of December he inclosed with a letter to Anderson a long set of "Instructions for my manager" which were to be "most strictly and pointedly attended to and executed." He had rented one of the farms to Lawrence Lewis, also the mill and distillery, and was desirous of renting the fishery in order to have less work and fewer hands to attend to; in fact, "an entire new scene" was to be enacted. The instructions were exceedingly voluminous, consisting of thirty closely written folio pages, and they contain plans for the rotation of crops for several years, as well as specific directions regarding fencing, pasturage, composts, feeding stock, and a great variety of other subjects. In them one can find our Farmer's final opinions on certain phases of agriculture. To draw them up must have cost him days of hard labor and that he found the task wearing is indicated by the fact that in two places he uses the dates 1782 and 1783 when he obviously meant 1802 and 1803.

There was no hunting now nor any of those other active outdoor sports in which he had once delighted and excelled, while "Alas! our dancing days are no more." Happily he was able to ride and labor to the last, yet more and more of his time had to be spent quietly, much of it, we may well believe, upon the splendid broad veranda of his home.

Unimaginative and unromantic though he was, what visions must sometimes have swept through the brain of that simple farmer as he gazed down upon the broad shining river or beyond at the clustered Maryland hills glorified by the descending sun. Perchance in those visions he saw a youthful envoy braving hundreds of miles of savage wilderness on an errand from which the boldest might have shrunk without disgrace. Then with a handful of men in forest green it is given to that youth to put a Continent in hazard and to strike on the slopes of Laurel Hill the first blow in a conflict that is fought out upon the plains of Germany, in far away Bengal and on most of the Seven Seas. For an instant there rises the delirium of that fateful day with Braddock beside the ford of the Monongahela when

> "Down the long trail from the Fort to the ford,
> Naked and streaked, plunge a moccasined horde:
> Huron and Wyandot, hot for the bout;
> Shawnee and Ottawa, barring him out.

> "'Twixt the pit and the crest, 'twixt the rocks and the grass,
> Where the bush hides the foe and the foe holds the pass,
> Beaujeu and Pontiac, striving amain;
> Huron and Wyandot, jeering the slain,"

The years pass and the same figure grown older and more sedate is taking command of an army of peasantry at war with their King. Dorchester Heights, Brooklyn, Fort Washington, Trenton, Princeton, Brandywine, Valley Forge, Monmouth, Morristown, the sun of Yorktown; Green, Gates, Arnold, Morgan, Lee, Lafayette, Howe, Clinton, Cornwallis—what memories! Lastly, a Cincinnatus grown bent and gray in service leaves his farm to head his country's civil affairs and give confidence and stability to an infant government by his wisdom and character.

Here, with bared heads, let us take leave of him—a farmer, but "the greatest of good men and the best of great men."

THE END